PRAISE FOR MOUTHFUL OF BIRDS

LONGLISTED FOR THE MAN BOOKER INTERNATIONAL PRIZE, 2019

A Most Anticipated Book According To
Vogue, Vanity Fair, The Millions, Huffington Post, Nylon, Literary Hub, Book Riot & Remezcla

'This is our world, and sharp-focused, but stripped of its usual meanings... Brutal violence is twisted into horrific, intensely experienced art.'
Guardian

'Chilling short stories by the Argentine author of *Fever Dream* confirm her as a master of the macabre... The finest offerings here beg to be illustrated by Paula Rego then animated by David Lynch – only two fellow masters of the macabre could do Schweblin's work justice.'
Financial Times

'Delving into the cryptic depths of the human psyche, this is a highly imaginative and thought-provoking collection, deftly translated by Megan McDowell.'
Observer

'To read Samanta Schweblin is to feel almost physically something unseen and nasty brush against your skin... These are fictions of indisputable power.'
Daily Telegraph

'In this slim and superb book, Schweblin takes on the desire to love, to parent, and to care for one's own body – hardly extraordinary themes – and invests them with a fresh poignancy.'
Vogue, Most Anticipated Books of 2019

'At once fantastically out there and real to the point of being haunting.'
Vanity Fair

'Fabulous... An eerie blend of the supernatural and the all too real.'
Daily Mail

be peculiar, the form is meticulous. The collection is chock-full of masterful reversals, last-minute turns that showcase Schweblin's ability to carry a story to a satisfying close... Thrilling.'

Chicago Review of Books

'These fabulist half-light tales leave some elements tantalisingly unsaid or off-page, but are sharpened through her technique and clarity of prose.'

The List

'If you were a fan of *Fever Dream*, Schweblin's Man Booker International Prize-shortlisted nightmarish novella, brace yourself for this similarly surreal "unearthly" and "unsettling" collection of short stories.'

Huffington Post India

'A writer in full control on the page. Her language is economical, yet supremely effective at creating a tense, claustrophobic atmosphere; shadows lurk behind the words left unwritten, the sentences that refuse to reveal the hidden things just around the corner.'

New York Magazine

'Schweblin is back with this book of short stories, each more unnerving than the last, and all with the unique ability to leave you with that throbbing, pulsing feeling following an electric shock or a sleepless night or a solid scare or all of the above.'

Nylon

'Schweblin once again deploys a heavy dose of nightmare fuel in this frightening, addictive collection... Canny, provocative and profoundly unsettling.'

Publishers Weekly (starred review)

'Schweblin builds dense and uncanny worlds, probing the psychology of human relationships and the ways we perceive existence and interpret culture, with dark humour and sharp teeth... An unquestionably imaginative author.'

Kirkus

'Samanta has a unique, inventive voice, and her stories have this ability to veer off into strange and unexpected territories with sublime grace. I admire and envy this gift.'

Daniel Alarcón, author of *At Night We Walk in Circles*

PRAISE FOR *FEVER DREAM*

SHORTLISTED FOR THE MAN BOOKER
INTERNATIONAL PRIZE, 2017

'A book to read in one frantic sitting – bold, uncanny and utterly gripping.' *Observer* Best Fiction of 2017

'Transcends the sensational plot elements to achieve a powerful and humane vision.' *Financial Times* Best Books of 2017

'A gloriously creepy fable.' *Guardian* Best Fiction of 2017

'Dazzling, unforgettable, and deeply strange. I've never read anything like it.' *Evening Standard* Books of the Year

'Read this in a single sitting and by the end I could hardly breathe. It's a total mind-wrecker. Amazing. Thrilling.'
Max Porter, author of *Grief is the Thing with Feathers*

'Explosive...delivers a skin-prickling masterclass in dread and suspense.' *The Economist* Best Books of 2017

'Punches far above its weight… The sort of book that makes you look under the bed last thing at night and sleep with the light on.' *Daily Mail*

'Each layer is soaked in dread, and the dread goes so deep that it works even on the third reading.' *London Review of Books*

'Genius.' *The New Yorker*

'Samanta Schweblin's novella is a skilfully paced and intricate omen that tears not just at ecological anxieties but at the core of maternal love.' *Times Literary Supplement*

MOUTHFUL OF BIRDS

STORIES

SAMANTA SCHWEBLIN

Translated by Megan McDowell

ONEWORLD

A Oneworld Book

First published in Great Britain and Australia
by Oneworld Publications, 2019
This paperback edition published 2019

Originally published, in Spanish and in somewhat different form, as *Pájaros en la boca*
by Random House Mondadori in 2010

Published by arrangement with Riverhead Books, an imprint of Penguin Publishing Group,
a division of Penguin Random House LLC

Copyright © 2010, 2019 by Samanta Schweblin
English translation copyright © 2019 by Megan McDowell

The moral right of Samanta Schweblin to be identified as the Author of this work has been
asserted by her in accordance with the Copyright, Designs and Patents Act 1988

ISBN 978-1-78607-669-4
eISBN 978-1-78607-457-7

Printed and bound in Great Britain by Clays Ltd, Elcograf S.p.A.

This is a work of fiction. While, as in all fiction, the literary perceptions and insights are based
on experience, all names, characters, places, and incidents either are products of the author's
imagination or are used fictitiously.

Oneworld Publications
10 Bloomsbury Street
London WC1B 3SR
United Kingdom

MIX
Paper from
responsible sources
FSC® C018072

To my grandparents Susana Soro and Alfredo de Vincenzo

CONTENTS

HEADLIGHTS

When she reaches the road, Felicity understands her fate. He has not waited for her, and, as if the past were a tangible thing, she thinks she can still see the weak reddish glow of the car's taillights fading on the horizon. In the flat darkness of the countryside, there is only disappointment, a wedding dress, and a bathroom she shouldn't have taken so long in.

Sitting on a rock beside the door, she picks grains of rice from the embroidery on her dress, with nothing to look at but the open fields, the highway, and, beside the highway, a women's bathroom.

Time passes during which Felicity throws off all the grains of rice. She still doesn't cry; deep in the shock of abandonment, she smooths the folds of her dress, examines her nails, and, as though expecting a return, stares out at the highway down which he disappeared.

"They don't come back," says Nené, and Felicity screams in fright. "The highway is shit."

The woman is behind Felicity, and she lights a cigarette. "Just shit, the very worst kind."

Felicity gets control of herself, and as the shock dies down, she rearranges her straps.

"First time?" asks Nené, and she waits unappreciatively for Felicity to regain enough courage to stop trembling and look at her. "I'm asking if the guy is your first husband."

Felicity forces a smile. She discovers in Nené the old and bitter face of a woman who was surely once more beautiful than Felicity herself. Amid the marks of premature old age, clear eyes and perfectly proportioned lips still remain.

"Yes, the first," says Felicity, with that shyness that turns the sound of a voice inward.

A white light appears on the highway, illuminates them as it passes, and vanishes, glowing red.

"So? You going to wait for him?" asks Nené.

Felicity looks at the highway, at the side where, if her

husband was to return, she would see the car appear. She can't bring herself to reply.

"Look," says Nené, "I'll make this short because there's really not much to it." She steps on the cigarette, emphasizing the words: "They get tired of waiting and they leave you. It seems waiting wears them out."

Felicity carefully follows the movement of a new cigarette toward the woman's mouth, the smoke that blends with the darkness, the lips that press the cigarette.

"So the girls cry and wait for them . . ." Nené goes on, "and they wait . . . And especially, the whole time they're waiting: they cry, cry, and cry."

Felicity's eyes stop following the cigarette. Right when she most needs sisterly support, when only another woman could understand what she is feeling in front of a women's bathroom beside the highway after being wholly abandoned by her new husband, she has only this arrogant woman who has been talking to her, and who is now shouting.

"And they keep crying and crying at all hours, every minute of every damned night!"

Felicity takes a deep breath, and her eyes fill with tears.

"And screw all that crying and crying . . . I'll tell you something. This is it. We're sick and tired of hearing about your stupid problems. We, little miss . . . What did you say your name was?"

Felicity wants to say *Felicity*, but she knows that if she opens her mouth, the only sound will be uncontrollable sobbing.

"Hello . . . your name was . . . ?"

Then the sobbing is uncontrollable.

"Fe . . . li . . ." Felicity tries to control herself, and though she doesn't really succeed, she does finish the word: ". . . city."

"Well, Feli-city, I was saying that we can't keep putting up with this situation. It's unsustainable, Feli-city!"

After she takes a long and noisy breath, Felicity's sobs start to swell again, dampening her entire face, which trembles as she breathes and shakes her head.

"I can't believe . . ." she gasps, "that he's . . ."

Nené stands up. She crushes her unfinished cigarette on the bathroom wall, looks at Felicity with contempt, and walks away.

"Rude!" Felicity shouts at her.

But a few seconds later, once she realizes she'll be left alone, Felicity catches up with Nené out in the field.

"Wait . . . Don't leave, you have to understand . . ."

Nené stops and looks at her.

"Shut up," says Nené, and she lights another cigarette. "Shut up, I'm telling you. Listen."

Felicity stops crying, chokes down something like the beginnings of another outbreak of sorrow.

There's a moment of silence during which Nené does not feel relief. Even more nervous and distraught than before, she says:

"Okay, now listen. Do you hear it?" Nené looks out at the black field.

Felicity is quiet and she concentrates, but she cannot hear anything. Nené shakes her head in disapproval.

"You cried too much, now you have to wait for your ears to get used to it."

Felicity looks off toward the fields and cocks her head a bit.

"They're crying . . ." says Felicity, in a low, almost ashamed voice.

"Yes. They're crying. Yes! They're crying! They cry all the damned night!" Nené gestures to her face: "Can't you see my face? When do we sleep? Never! All we do is listen to them every damned night. And we're not going to take it anymore, understand?"

Felicity looks at her, startled. In the fields, voices of wailing and plaintive women repeat the names of their husbands over and over.

"And they all cry!" says Nené.

Then the voices begin to shout:

Psycho!

Miserable, unfeeling bitch!

And other voices join in:

Let us cry, you hysterical shrew!

Nené looks furiously all around her. She shouts into the fields:

"And what about us, you cowards . . . ? Some of us have been here more than forty years, abandoned same as you, and we have to hear your stupid little problems every damned night? Huh? What about us?"

There's a silence, and Felicity looks at Nené in fear.

Take a pill! Crazy woman!

Although they're out in the fields they can still see the highway. Parallel to where they are standing, a pair of white lights pulls up beside the little building.

"Another one," says Nené, and as if this were the last thing she could bear, she drops to the ground, exhausted.

"Another one?" asks Felicity. "Another woman? But . . . is he going to leave her? Maybe he'll wait . . ."

Nené bites her lips and shakes her head. In the fields the cries grow ever more unfriendly.

Come on, you hussy, let's see you show your face . . .

Come on, now that you don't have your little rebel friends . . .

Feeble old hag . . .

Felicity takes Nené's hand and tries to pull her up, pointing toward the bathroom.

"We have to do something! We have to warn that poor woman!" says Felicity.

But then she stops and falls silent, because Felicity has seen the exact image of her painful recent past: the car driving off before the woman who got out has had the chance to get back in, and the lights, previously white and bright, disappear, reddish, in the other direction.

"He left," says Felicity, "he left without her."

6

Like Nené did before, she lets her body collapse to the ground. Nené rests her hand on Felicity's.

"That's how it always is, dear." Nené pats Felicity's hand. "It's inevitable. On the highway, at least . . . Always."

"But . . ." says Felicity.

"Always," says Nené.

Where are you, slut? Say something!

Felicity looks at Nené and understands how much bigger this woman's sadness is than her own.

Sorry ass tramp!

Ugly old bitch!

"Leave her alone!" says Felicity.

She moves closer to Nené and hugs her like a little girl.

Oh . . . Scary! says a voice. *So now you've got a little sidekick . . .*

"I'm not anyone's sidekick," says Felicity. "I'm just trying to help . . ."

Oh . . . she's only trying to help . . .

"Shut up!" says Nené.

You all know why she was left on the highway?

Because she's a skinny walrus!

No, she got left because—laughter—*because while she was trying on her little wedding dress, we were already gettin' it on with her man . . .*

The laughter is closer now; it completely drowns out the crying. From the bathroom, a figure is walking, slowly, toward Nené and Felicity.

Look, here comes another one . . . tramp!

As the figure comes closer they discover the face of an old woman. Every few steps, she turns and looks at the highway. She is dressed in golden tones, and from her neckline peeks the sensual black lace of lingerie. Once she is close, before she can ask questions, Felicity cuts her off:

"Always. Always on the highway, Grandmother."

When the old woman sees them, sitting in the field in their wedding dresses, she straightens and looks indignantly toward the road.

"But how——?"

Felicity interrupts her:

"Don't cry, please," says Felicity. "Don't make things worse."

"But it can't be . . ." says the old woman, and in her disappointment, her hand opens and a marriage certificate falls to the ground.

She looks contemptuously at the highway down which the car has disappeared, and says, "Scoundrel! Impotent old coot!"

Come on, hussy!

"Why don't you shut up, you windbags!" shouts Nené, and she gets brusquely to her feet.

The old woman looks at her in fright.

"Old biddies!" Nené goes on.

We're gonna get you, you snake!

Trying to understand, the old woman looks at Felicity, who,

like Nené, has stood up and is anxiously peering into the darkness of the fields.

Show your face, come on, the women's voices can be heard ever closer.

Felicity and Nené look at each other. Beneath their feet they feel the ground tremble as hundreds of desperate women advance through the field.

"What's happening?" asks the old woman. "Who are those voices, what do they want?" She kneels down and picks up the marriage certificate. Like Felicity and Nené, she backs toward the highway without turning around, without taking her eyes from the black mass in the dark fields that seems to be moving closer and closer to them.

"How many are there?" asks Felicity.

"A lot," says Nené. "Too many."

There are so many curses and insults coming from so close by that it's useless to respond or try to placate them.

"What should we do?" asks Felicity. The three of them back up faster and faster.

"Don't even think about crying," says Nené.

The old woman, clutching at her wedding dress and wrinkling it in one nervous hand, grasps Felicity's arm with her other.

"Don't be scared, Grandmother, it's okay," says Felicity.

But the taunting is so loud now that the old woman can't hear her words. On the highway, off in the distance, a white dot grows like a new ray of hope. Perhaps this is the moment when Felicity thinks, for the last time, of love. Perhaps she thinks to herself: *Don't let him leave her; don't let him abandon her.*

"If it stops, we get in," shouts Nené.

"What did she say?" asks the grandmother. They are close to the bathroom now.

"That if the car stops—" says Felicity.

"What?" asks the grandmother.

The murmur is converging on them. They can't see anyone, but they know the women are there, just a few yards away. Felicity screams. Something like hands brush against her legs, her neck, her fingertips. Felicity screams and she doesn't hear Nené, who has moved farther away and is telling her to grab the old woman and run. The car stops in front of the bathroom. Nené turns back toward Felicity and tells her to move, to drag the grandmother with her. But it's the grandmother who reacts and drags Felicity toward Nené, who is already next to the car and waiting for the woman to get out so she can get in herself and order the man to drive.

"They won't let go!" screams Felicity. "They won't let go of me!" And she desperately tries to break free of the last hands holding her back.

The old woman pulls. She yanks on Felicity with all her strength. Nené is waiting anxiously for the door to open, for the woman to get out. But the one who emerges is the man. With the headlights shining on the road, he still hasn't seen the women, and he gets out in a hurry while he fumbles for the zipper of his pants. Then the din grows. The laughing, taunting voices forget Nené and fixate purely and exclusively on him. They reach his ears. In the man's eyes, the fear of a rabbit facing the furies. By the time he stops, it's too late. Nené has gone around and gotten into the man's seat. She restrains the woman, who is trying to escape, and she opens a back door for Felicity and the grandmother.

"Hold her," says Nené, and she lets go of the woman to leave her in the grandmother's hands. The old woman obeys the order wordlessly.

"If she wants to get out, let her," says Felicity. "Maybe these two do love each other and it's not for us to stand in their way."

The newcomer wiggles free of the old lady but she doesn't get out of the car. She asks, "What do you want? Where did you come from?"—one question after another, until Nené opens the passenger door.

"Get out, quick," she says.

They can hear the women's cries even once they're in the car, and in front of them, detached from the darkness by the headlights, stands the frozen, terrified figure of a man who is not thinking about the same thing he was a minute ago.

"No way am I getting out," says the newcomer. She looks at the man without tenderness, and then at Nené: "Get going before he comes back," she says, and she locks the door from inside.

Nené puts the car in drive. The man hears the noise and turns to look at them.

"Go!" shouts the newcomer.

The old lady claps nervously, then squeezes Felicity's hand; Felicity looks fearfully at the man as he approaches. The tires on one side are off the road, and the car skids in the mud. Nené turns the steering wheel wildly, and for a moment the car's headlights shine into the fields. But what they see then is not precisely the fields: the car's light is lost in the immensity of the night, but it's enough to distinguish in the darkness the swarming mass of hundreds of women. They're running toward the car. Or, more accurately, toward the man standing in front of the car, waiting motionlessly for them, as though for death.

The newcomer presses her own foot down on Nené's to floor the accelerator. And with the image framed in the rearview mirror of the crowd of women falling upon the man, Nené manages to get the car back on the road. The motor drowns out the shouts and insults, and soon all is silence and darkness.

The newcomer shifts in her seat.

"I never loved him," she says. "When he got out of the car, I thought about taking the wheel and leaving him by the side of the road. But I don't know, the maternal instinct . . ."

None of the other women are listening. All of them, and now the newcomer, too, just look out at the highway and are silent for a while. That's when it happens.

"It can't be," says Nené.

In front of them, in the distance, the horizon starts to light up with small pairs of white lights.

"What?" asks the grandmother. "What's going on?"

In the passenger seat, the newcomer throws glances at Nené, as if waiting for an explanation. The pairs of lights grow, coming closer. Felicity peers between the two front seats.

"They're coming back," she says. She smiles and looks at Nené.

On the highway, the first pairs of lights are now cars, almost on top of them, and now they pass at full speed.

"They changed their minds," says Felicity. "It's them, they're coming back for us!"

"No," says Nené.

She lights a cigarette and then, exhaling smoke, she adds:

"It's them, yes. But they're coming back for him."

PRESERVES

A week passes, a month, and we gradually start accepting that Teresita will be here ahead of all our plans. I'll have to turn down my scholarship, because in a few months it won't be easy for me to keep studying. Maybe not because of Teresita, maybe it's just anxiety, but I can't stop eating and I start getting fatter. Manuel carries the food to me on the sofa, in bed, in the yard. Everything arranged on the tray, tidy in the kitchen, stocked in the pantry, as if the guilt, or whatever it is, was driving him to meet my every expectation. But he's losing energy, and he doesn't seem very happy: he comes home late, doesn't keep me company, doesn't like to talk about it.

Another month passes. Mom resigns herself, too, buys us some gifts and gives them to us—I know her well—a bit sadly. She says:

"Here is a washable diaper bag with a Velcro closure . . . These are pure cotton ankle socks . . . Here's the piqué hooded towel . . ." Dad watches her and nods.

"Oh, I don't know . . ." I say, and I don't know if I'm referring to the gifts or to Teresita. "The truth is, I just don't know," I say later to my mother-in-law when she drops by with a set of little colored sheets. "I don't know," I say, not really knowing what to say, and I hug the sheets and burst into tears.

The third month I feel sadder still. Every time I get up I stand for a while in front of the mirror. My face, my arms, my whole body, and especially my belly are more swollen. Sometimes I call Manuel in and ask him to stand beside me. He, in contrast, looks thinner. He seems distracted. He doesn't talk much. He comes home from work and sits down to watch television, his head in his hands. It's not that he loves me any less. I know that Manuel adores me and I know that, like me, he has nothing against our little Teresita—what could he have against her? It's just that there was so much to do before she came.

Sometimes Mom asks if she can touch my belly. I sit on the sofa and she talks to Teresita in a soft and loving voice. Manuel's mom, on the other hand, tends to call all the time to ask how I'm doing, where I am, what I'm eating, how I feel, and anything else she can think of to ask me.

I have insomnia. I spend nights lying in bed awake, looking at the ceiling with my hands over little Teresita. I can't think about anything else. I don't understand it—there are so many things in this world that seem marvelous to me, like renting a car in one country and returning it in another, thawing out a fresh fish that died thirty days ago, or paying bills without leaving the house. How is it possible that in a world like that, we can't just make a small change in the order of events? I just can't resign myself.

Then I stop worrying about what insurance will cover and start looking for other alternatives. I talk to obstetricians, healers, and even a shaman. Someone gives me a midwife's number and I talk to her over the phone. But they all, in their own ways, present conformist or perverse solutions that have nothing to do with what I'm looking for. It's hard for me to get used to the idea of receiving Teresita so early, but I don't want to hurt her, either. And then I find Dr. Weisman.

The doctor's office is on the top floor of an old building downtown. There's no secretary, no waiting room. Just a small entrance hall and two rooms. Weisman is very friendly as he ushers us in and offers us coffee. During our conversation he is especially interested in what kind of family we are—our parents, our marriage, the individual relationships between all of us. We answer every question he asks. Weisman interlaces his fingers and rests his hands on the desk, seemingly satisfied with our profile. He tells us a few things about his career, the success of his research and what he can offer us, but he realizes he doesn't need to convince us, and he moves on to explain the treatment. Every once in a while I look at Manuel: he is listening attentively, nodding; he seems enthusiastic. The plan includes changes in diet and sleep patterns, breathing exercises, medicine. We're going to have to talk to Mom and Dad, and with Manuel's mother; their roles are important, too. I write everything down in my notebook, point by point.

"And what guarantee do we have with this treatment?" I ask.

"We have what we need for everything to turn out well," says Weisman.

The next day Manuel stays home. We sit at the living room table, surrounded by graphs and papers, and get to work. I write down as faithfully as possible how things have happened from the first moment we suspected that Teresita had come early. We summon our parents and we are clear with them: the matter is decided, the treatment is under way, and there is nothing to discuss. Dad is about to ask a question, but Manuel interrupts him.

"You have to do what we ask," he says, and he looks at them as though imploring them to commit, "on the right day and at the right time."

I understand what he's feeling: we're taking this seriously and we expect the same from them. They are worried, and I think they'll never really understand what it's all about, but they promise to follow the instructions, and each of them goes home with a list.

When the first ten days are over, things are already running a little more smoothly. I take my three pills a day on time, and I respect every session of "conscious breathing." Conscious breathing is a fundamental part of the treatment, and it's an innovative method of relaxation and concentration, discovered and taught by Weisman himself. Sitting on the grass out in the yard, I focus on making contact with the "damp womb of the earth." I start by inhaling once and exhaling twice. I draw out my breath until my inhale is five seconds long and my exhale is eight. After several days of practice, I inhale for ten seconds and exhale for fifteen. Then I move to the second level of conscious breathing, where I start to feel the direction of my energies. Weisman says this level is going to take more time, but he insists the exercise is within my reach and that I have to keep working at it. There comes a moment when it's possible to visualize the speed of the energy as it circulates through the body. It feels like a gentle tickle and it generally starts in the lips, hands, and feet. You have to try to slow it down, gradually. The goal is to stop it entirely and, little by little, start it circulating again in the opposite direction.

Manuel can't be very affectionate with me yet. He has to be faithful to the plan we made, and so for a month and a half he has to stay away, talk only when necessary, and come home late some nights. He complies diligently, but I know him: I know that secretly he's better, that he's dying to hug me and tell me how much he misses me. But that's how things must be done for now; we can't risk straying from the script for even a second.

The next month I keep progressing with conscious breathing. Now I almost feel like I can stop the energy. Weisman says it won't be long now, I only have to push a little more. He ups the dosage of my pills. I start to feel my anxiety diminish, and I'm eating a little less. Following the first point on her list, Manuel's mother makes her greatest effort and tries, gradually—that part is important and we underline it many times: *gradually*, it says—to start making fewer calls to our house, and to not be so eager to talk about Teresita all the time.

The second month is perhaps the one with the most changes. My body is not as swollen now, and to both of our surprise and joy, my belly starts to shrink. This change, so marked, alerts our parents. Maybe it's only now that they understand, or intuit, what the treatment is about. Manuel's mother, especially, seems to fear the worst, and although she tries to stay on the sidelines and keep to her list, I feel her fear and her doubt and I worry it will affect the treatment.

I start sleeping better at night, and I don't feel as depressed anymore. I tell Weisman about my progress in conscious breathing. He gets excited, it seems I'm about to reverse my energy—I'm so, so close, a hairsbreadth from the goal.

The third month starts, the penultimate. It's the month when our parents will play their biggest roles; we're anxious to make sure they keep their word so that everything comes out perfectly. They do, and they do it well, and we are grateful. Manuel's mother comes over one afternoon and reclaims the colored sheets she'd brought for Teresita. Maybe because she had thought about this detail for a long time, she asks me for a bag to wrap the package in. "It's just that that's how I brought it over," she says, "in a bag, so that's how it should go," and she winks at us. Then it's my parents' turn. They also come for their gifts, reclaim them one by one: first the hooded piqué towel, then the pure cotton socks, finally the washable diaper bag with the Velcro closure. I wrap them up. Mom asks if she can caress my belly one last time. I sit on the sofa and she sits next to me, talking in her soft and loving voice. She strokes my belly and says, "This is my Teresita, how I'm going to miss my Teresita." I don't say anything, but I know that if she could have, if she didn't have to stick to her list, she would have cried.

The days of the last month pass quickly. Manuel can come closer now, and the truth is, his company does me good. We stand before the mirror and laugh. The feeling is the total opposite of what you feel when you're leaving on a trip. It's not the joy of leaving, but of staying. It's adding another year to the best year of your life, and under the same conditions. It's the chance to keep on, unchanged.

I'm much less swollen now. It's a physical relief and it raises my spirits. I visit Weisman for the last time.

"We're getting close," he says, and he pushes the preservation jar across the desk, toward me.

It's cold, and it needs to stay that way; that's why I brought the thermal lunchbox, as Weisman recommended. I have to store it in the freezer as soon as I get home. I pick it up: the liquid is transparent but thick, like a jar of clear amber.

One morning, during a session of conscious breathing, I make it to the final level: I breathe slowly, my body feels the earth's dampness and the energy that surrounds it. I breathe once, then again, and again, and then everything stops. The energy seems to materialize around me and I can specify the exact moment when, little by little, it starts to turn in the opposite direction. It's a purifying feeling, rejuvenating, as if water or air were returning of their own accord to the place where they were once contained.

Then the day arrives. It's marked on the refrigerator calendar; Manuel circled it in red when we came back from Weisman's office the first time. I don't know when it will happen, and I'm worried. Manuel is at home. I'm lying in bed. I hear him pacing, restless. I touch my belly. It's a normal belly, like that of any other woman—it's not a pregnant belly, I mean. Weisman says the treatment was very intense: I'm a little anemic, and much thinner than before the episode with Teresita started.

I wait all morning and all afternoon locked in the bedroom. I don't want to eat, or come out, or talk. Manuel looks in every once in a while and asks how I'm doing. I imagine Mom must be climbing the walls, but they all know they can't call or stop by to see me.

I've been feeling nauseated for a while now. My stomach burns and throbs more and more intensely, as if it were going to explode. I have to tell Manuel. I try to stand up but I can't; I hadn't realized how dizzy I am. I have to tell Manuel to call Weisman. For a moment I manage to get up. I pause and then fall to my knees. I think about conscious breathing, but my head has already moved on to something else. I'm afraid. I'm scared something will go wrong and we'll hurt Teresita. Maybe she knows what's happening; maybe this whole thing is all wrong. Manuel comes into the room and runs to me.

"I just want to leave it until later . . ." I tell him. "I don't want . . ."

I want to tell him to leave me here on the floor, that it doesn't matter, he should run and call Weisman, that everything has gone wrong. But I can't talk. My body is shaking; I've lost control over it. Manuel kneels down next to me, takes my hands, talks to me. I can't hear what he's saying. I feel like I'm going to throw up. I cover my mouth. He reacts then, and he leaves me alone and runs to the kitchen. He's gone only a few seconds; he comes back with the disinfected jar and the plastic case that says "Dr. Weisman." He breaks the safety seal on the container, pours the clear liquid into the jar. I feel like throwing up again, but I can't, I don't want to: not yet. I heave, again and again. I gag more and more violently and it's hard to breathe. For the

23

first time I think of the possibility of death. I think about it for a second and then I can't breathe at all. Manuel watches me, unsure what to do. The gagging stops and something catches in my throat. I close my mouth and grab Manuel by the wrist. Then I feel something small, the size of an almond. I hold it on my tongue; it's fragile. I know what I have to do but I can't do it. It's an unmistakable sensation that will stay with me for years. I look at Manuel, and he seems to accept the time I need. *She'll wait for us*, I think. *She'll be okay, until the time is right*. Then he hands me the jar, and finally, gently, I spit her out.

BUTTERFLIES

"You'll see, my girl is wearing such a pretty dress today," Calderón says to Gorriti. "It looks so nice on her with those brown eyes she has—its color, you know. And those little feet . . ." They're standing with the other parents, waiting anxiously for their children to be let out. Calderón is talking; Gorriti is looking at the still-locked doors. "You'll see," says Calderón. "Stay here, you have to stick close because they're about to come out. And yours, how's he?" The other man pantomimes pain and points to his teeth. "You don't say," says Calderón. "And did you do the tooth fairy? With mine it's no good, she's too smart." Gorriti looks at the clock. The doors will open any second now and the children will burst out, laughing and shouting in a tumult of colors, some spotted with paint or chocolate. But for some reason the bell is delayed. The parents wait.

A brownish butterfly lands on Calderón's arm and he quickly traps it. The creature struggles to get away, but he presses its wings together and holds it by the ends. He squeezes hard so it can't escape. "You'll see, you just have to see her," he tells Gorriti as he shakes it, "she's just adorable." But he presses so hard he starts to feel the tips of the wings sticking together. He slides his fingers down and sees that he has marked them. The butterfly tries to get free, fluttering its wings, and one of them splits down the middle like paper. Calderón is sorry, tries to hold it still so he can get a good look at the damage, but he ends up with part of the wing stuck to one of his fingers. Gorriti watches him with disgust and shakes his head, gestures for him to drop it. Calderón lets go. The butterfly falls to the ground. It moves awkwardly, tries to fly but no longer can. It finally stays still, flapping one of its wings every now and then, but it doesn't try anything more. Gorriti tells him to finish it off once and for all, and Calderón, for the butterfly's own good, of course, stomps on it.

He doesn't even have time to lift his foot when he realizes something strange is happening. He looks toward the doors and then, as if a sudden wind had breached the locks, the doors open and hundreds of butterflies of every color and size rush out toward the waiting parents. He thinks they might attack him; maybe he thinks he's going to die. The other parents don't seem to be afraid, and the butterflies just flutter among them. The last one comes out, lagging behind the others, and joins them.

Calderón stands looking at the open doors and through the windows of the main hall, at the silent classrooms. Some parents are still crowding in front of the doors and shouting the names of their children. Then the butterflies, all of them in just a few seconds, fly off in different directions. The parents try to catch them.

Calderón, on the other hand, stands motionless. He can't bring himself to lift his foot from the one he has killed. He is, perhaps, afraid of recognizing his girl's colors in its dead wings.

MOUTHFUL OF BIRDS

I turned off the TV and looked out the window. Silvia's car was parked in front of my house, its emergency lights blinking. As I stood there wondering whether there was any real possibility of not answering the door, the bell rang again: she knew I was home. I went to the door and opened it.

"Silvia."

"Hello," she said, and came inside before I could get another word out. "We have to talk."

She pointed me to my own sofa and I obeyed, because some-times, when the past knocks at the door and treats me like the past four years haven't happened, it turns out I'm still a dumbass.

"You're not going to like this. It's . . . It's intense." She looked at her watch. "It's about Sara."

"It's always about Sara," I said.

"You'll just say I'm exaggerating, and that I'm crazy and all that. But there's no time today. You're coming home with me right now, you've got to see this with your own eyes."

"What's wrong?"

"Plus, I told Sara you were coming, so she's waiting for you."

We sat in silence a moment. I was wondering what the next step would be, until she frowned, stood up, and walked to the door. I picked up my coat and followed her out.

From outside the house looked the same as always, the lawn newly mown and Silvia's azaleas hanging from the second-floor balconies. We both got out of our cars and went inside without exchanging a word. Sara was sitting on the sofa. Although she'd finished classes for the year, she was wearing her high school uniform. The way she filled it out, she looked like those porno schoolgirls in magazines. She was sitting straight up, legs to-gether and her hands on her knees, focusing on some point on the window or out in the yard like she was doing one of her mother's yoga exercises. She had always been fairly pale and thin, but now she seemed to be brimming with health. Her legs and arms looked stronger, as if she'd been working out for several months. Her hair shone and her cheeks were slightly flushed, like blush but real. When she saw me come in she smiled and said:

"Hi, Dad."

Although my little girl really was a sweetheart, two words were all it took for me to realize that something was really off with the kid, and I was sure it had something to do with her mother. Sometimes I think I should have brought her to live with me, but I almost always think otherwise. Not far from the TV, beside the window, there was a cage. It was a birdcage—maybe a foot and a half tall—that hung from the ceiling, empty.

"What's that?"

"A cage," Sara said, and smiled.

Silvia motioned for me to follow her to the kitchen. We stood by the window and she checked to make sure Sara wasn't listening. The girl was still sitting bolt upright on the sofa, looking out toward the street as if we'd never arrived. Silvia spoke to me in a low voice.

"Look, you're going to have to take this calmly."

"Come on, Silvia, stop jerking me around. What's going on?"

"I haven't fed her since yesterday."

"Are you kidding me?"

"So you'll see with your own eyes."

"Uh-huh . . . Are you crazy?"

She told me to follow her back to the living room, where she pointed me to the sofa. I sat down across from Sara. Silvia left the house, and we saw her cross in front of the window and go into the garage.

"What's going on with your mom?"

Sara shrugged her shoulders. Her straight black hair was pulled back into a ponytail, and she had thick bangs that hung down almost over her eyes.

Silvia returned with a shoe box. She carried it level, in both hands, as if it held something delicate. She went to the birdcage and opened it, then took from the shoe box a very small sparrow, the size of a golf ball; she put the bird into the cage and closed it. She dropped the box to the floor and kicked it to one side, where it lay with another nine or ten similar boxes under the desk. Then Sara got up, her ponytail shining and bouncing, and skipped over to the cage like a little girl five years younger. With her back to us, standing on her tiptoes, she opened the cage and took out the bird. I couldn't see what she did. The bird screeched and she struggled a moment, maybe because it was trying to escape. Silvia covered her mouth with her hand. When Sara turned back to us, the bird wasn't there anymore. Her mouth, nose, chin, and both hands were smeared with blood. She smiled sheepishly. Her gigantic mouth arched and opened, and her red teeth made me jump to my feet. I ran to the bathroom, locked the door, and vomited into the toilet. I thought Silvia would follow me and start laying blame and ordering me around from the other side of the door, but she didn't. I rinsed my mouth and face and stood in front of the mirror, listening. I heard them carry something heavy down the stairs. The front door opened and closed a few times. Sara asked if she could have the photo that was on the shelf. Silvia said yes, and her voice was already distant. I came out of the bathroom trying not to make noise, and I peered into the hallway. The front door was wide open, and Silvia was loading the birdcage into the backseat of my car. I took a few steps with the intention of going outside and shouting a few choice things, but Sara came out of the kitchen and onto the street, and I stopped short so she wouldn't see me. They hugged. Silvia kissed her and put her into the passenger seat. I waited until she'd come back inside and closed the door.

"What the hell?"

"You're taking her."

She went to the desk and started to flatten and fold the empty boxes.

"My god, Silvia, your daughter eats birds!"

"I can't do it anymore."

"She eats birds! Have you taken her to the doctor? What in hell does she do with the bones?"

Silvia stood looking at me, disconcerted.

"I guess she swallows them, too. I don't know if birds . . ." she said, and she stood looking at me.

"I can't take her."

"One more day with her and I'll kill myself. I'll kill her, and then I'll kill myself."

"She eats birds!"

Silvia went into the bathroom and locked the door. I looked out through the picture window. Sara waved happily to me from the car. I tried to calm down. I tried to come up with something that would help me take a few stumbling steps toward the door, praying that in the time it took to reach it I would go back to being an ordinary man, a fastidious and organized guy who was capable of spending ten minutes in front of a shelf of cans in the supermarket, making sure the peas he's buying are really the most suitable ones. I thought about how, considering there are people who eat people, eating live birds wasn't so bad. Also, from a natural point of view it was healthier than drugs, and from a social one, it was easier to hide than a pregnancy at thirteen. But I'm pretty sure that until I reached for the car door handle I went on thinking, *She eats birds, she eats birds, she eats birds*, on and on.

I brought Sara home. She didn't say anything on the way, and when we got there, she unloaded her things by herself. Her birdcage, her suitcase—which she and her mother had loaded into the trunk—and four shoe boxes like the one Silvia had brought from the garage. I couldn't bring myself to help her. I opened the front door, and I waited there while she came and went with everything. After I'd told her she could use the upstairs bedroom and waited a few minutes while she settled in, I had her come down and sit across from me at the dining table. I fixed two cups of coffee. Sara pushed hers to the side and said she didn't drink anything brewed.

"You eat birds, Sara."

"Yes, Dad."

She bit her lips, ashamed, and said:

"You do, too."

"You eat *live* birds, Sara."

"Yes, Dad."

I remembered Sara at five years old, sitting at the table with us and fanatically devouring a squash, and I thought we would find the way to resolve this problem. But when the Sara I had in front of me smiled again, I wondered what it would be like to have a mouth full of something all feathers and feet, to swallow something warm and moving. I covered my mouth with my hand the way Silvia had done earlier, and I left Sara alone before the two untouched cups of coffee.

Three days passed. Sara spent almost all that time in the living room, upright on the sofa with her legs pressed together and her hands on her knees. I left early for work and endured the hours searching the internet for infinite combinations of words like *bird*, *raw*, *cure*, *adoption*, knowing that she was still sitting there, looking out at the yard for hours on end. When I came back to the house around seven and saw her just as I'd pictured her throughout the day, the hair stood up on the back of my neck and I felt like leaving and locking her in, hermetically sealed, like those insects I'd hunted when I was little and kept in glass jars until the air ran out. Could I do it?

When I was little I went to a circus once, and I saw a bearded woman who put live rats in her mouth. She held one there for a while, its tail wriggling between her closed lips while she paraded before the audience, smiling, her eyes turned upward as if it gave her some great pleasure. Now I thought about that woman almost every night as I tossed and turned, unable to sleep, mulling over the possibility of checking Sara into a psychiatric hospital. Maybe I could visit her once or twice a week. Silvia and I could take turns. I thought about those cases when the doctors recommend the patient be isolated, keeping him away from family for a few months. Maybe it would be a good option for everyone, but I wasn't sure Sara could survive in a place like that. Or could she? In any case, her mother wouldn't allow it. Or would she? I couldn't decide.

On the fourth day Silvia came to see us. She brought five shoe boxes that she left just inside the front door. Neither of us said a word about them. She asked where Sara was, and I pointed her to the bedroom upstairs. Later, she came back down alone. I offered her coffee. We drank it in the living room, in silence. She was pale, and at times her hands shook and made the cup rattle in the saucer. We both knew what the other was thinking. I could have said, *This is your fault, this is what you've brought us to,* and she could have said something absurd like *This is happening because you never paid attention to her.* But the truth is, we were both very tired.

"I'll take care of that," said Silvia before she left, pointing to the shoe boxes she'd brought. I didn't say anything, but I was deeply grateful.

In the supermarket, people loaded their carts up with cereal boxes, sweets, vegetables, and dairy products. I stuck with my canned foods and waited quietly in the checkout line. I went to the supermarket two or three times a week. Sometimes, even if I had nothing to buy, I still stopped there on my way home. I took a cart and walked through the aisles thinking about what I could be forgetting. At night, we watched TV together. Sara sat upright in her corner of the couch, and I sat at the other end, sneaking a look at her every once in a while to see if she was following the show or had her eyes glued on the yard again. I fixed food for us both and brought it to the living room on two trays. I put Sara's down in front of her, and that's where it stayed. She waited for me to start eating and then said:

"Excuse me, Dad."

And she'd stand up, go to her room, and gently close the door. The first time, I turned down the TV and waited in silence. There was a brief, sharp shriek. A few seconds later, I heard the pipes in the bathroom, the water running. Sometimes she came down after a little while, serene, her hair perfectly combed. Other times she showered and came down in pajamas.

Sara didn't want to go out. Studying her behavior, I thought maybe she was suffering from the beginnings of agoraphobia. Sometimes I took a chair out to the yard and tried to convince her to come outside for a while. But it was no use. Even so, her complexion continued to radiate energy, and she looked more and more beautiful, as if she spent her days exercising in the sun.

Every once in a while, as I went about my business, I found a feather. On the floor beside the door, behind the coffee can, among the silverware, or in the bathroom sink, still wet. I would pick it up, taking care that she didn't see me do it, and flush it down the toilet. Sometimes I stood watching the water carry it down. Sometimes the toilet filled up again, the water grew calm and mirrorlike once more, and I was still there looking, wondering if it was necessary to go back to the supermarket, if it was really worth it to fill the carts with so much garbage, and thinking about Sara, about what could be out there in the yard.

One afternoon, Silvia called to let me know she was in bed with a vicious flu. She said she couldn't come visit us. She asked if I could manage without her. I asked if she had a fever, if she was eating enough, if she'd been to the doctor, and when I had her busy enough with her answers, I told her I had to hang up, and I did. The phone rang again, but I didn't answer.

We watched TV. When I brought my food, Sara didn't get up to go to her room. She concentrated on the yard until I finished eating, then she looked back at the TV show.

The next day, I stopped at the supermarket before going home. I put a few things in my cart, the same ones as always. I wandered the aisles as if I were doing a first reconnaissance of the store. I stopped at the pet section, where there was food for dogs, cats, rabbits, birds, and fish. I picked up some of the items and examined them more closely. I read their ingredients, how many calories they provided, and the amounts recommended for each breed, weight, and age. Then I went to the gardening section, where there were only plants with and without flowers, and flowerpots and dirt, so I went back to the pet section and stood there thinking about what to do next. Other shoppers filled their carts and steered them around me. The loudspeaker announced a sale on dairy products in honor of Mother's Day, and then played a song about a guy who had all kinds of women but who longed for his first love, until finally I pushed the cart back to the canned-goods section.

That night it took Sara a while to fall asleep. My room was below hers and I could hear her pace nervously above me, get into bed, and then get out again. I wondered what condition the room was in; I hadn't gone up since she'd arrived. Maybe the place was a real disaster, a barnyard full of muck and feathers.

The third night after Silvia's call, before I went home, I stopped to look in the birdcages hanging from a pet store's awning. None of the birds looked like the sparrow I'd seen at Silvia's house. They were all brightly colored, and in general a little bigger. I stood there for a while until a salesman came over to ask me if I was interested in any of the birds. I said no, absolutely not, that I was just looking. He stayed nearby, moving boxes around and looking out toward the street, and then he realized I really wasn't going to buy anything and he went back to the counter.

At home, Sara was waiting on the sofa, upright in her yoga position. We greeted each other.

"Hi, Sara."

"Hi, Dad."

Her rosy cheeks were fading, and she didn't look as healthy as she had on previous days. I made my food, sat down on the sofa, and turned on the TV. After a while Sara said:

"Daddy . . ."

I swallowed what I was chewing and turned down the volume on the TV, unsure whether she had really spoken, but there she was, her legs pressed together and her hands on her knees, looking at me.

"What?"

"Do you love me?"

I made a movement with my hand and accompanied it with a nod. The whole gesture together meant *Yes, of course*. She was my daughter, right? And just in case, thinking mostly about what my ex-wife would have considered "appropriate," I said:

"Yes, sweetheart. Of course."

And then Sara smiled and looked out at the yard for the rest of the TV show.

We slept badly again, Sara pacing her room end-to-end, me tossing and turning in bed until I finally drifted off. The next day I called Silvia. It was Saturday, but she didn't answer the phone. I called back later, and again around noon. I left a message. Sara spent the whole morning sitting on the sofa looking out at the yard. Her hair was a little disheveled and she wasn't sitting up so straight anymore; she looked very tired. I asked her if she was all right and she said:

"Yes, Dad."

"Why don't you go out to the yard for a while?"

"No, Dad."

Thinking of our conversation the night before, it occurred to me to ask if she loved me, but right away that struck me as pure stupidity. I called Silvia again. I left another message. In a low voice, making sure Sara couldn't hear me, I said to her voice mail:

"It's urgent, please."

We waited, each of us at our end of the sofa, with the TV on. A few hours later Sara said:

"Excuse me, Dad."

She went to her room and closed the door. I turned off the TV so I could hear better: Sara didn't make a noise. I decided I'd call Silvia one more time. I picked up the receiver, but when I heard the dial tone I hung up. I drove the car to the pet store, looked for a salesperson, and told him I needed a small bird, the smallest he had. The salesman opened a catalogue with photographs and said that prices and food varied from one species to the next.

"Do you like exotic species, or do you prefer more household ones?"

I pounded the counter with my open palm. Everything displayed on the counter jumped and the clerk was silent, looking at me. I pointed to a small, dark bird that was moving nervously from one side of its cage to another. They charged me a hundred twenty pesos and gave it to me in a square, green cardboard box with little holes poked through it, and on the lid, a pamphlet from the breeder with the photo of the bird. They also tried to give me a free bag of birdseed, but I turned it down.

When I got home Sara was still in her room. For the first time since she'd been in the house, I went upstairs and opened her door. She was sitting on the bed across from the open window. She looked at me. Neither of us said anything. She was so pale she looked sick. The room was clean and neat, the door to the bathroom ajar. There were some thirty shoe boxes in a neat pile on the desk, but flattened so they didn't take up so much space. The cage hung empty near the window. On the night table, next to the lamp, was the framed photo she'd brought from her mother's house. The bird moved and its feet scratched the cardboard, but Sara stayed still. I placed the box on the desk, and without a word I left the room and closed the door. Then I realized I didn't feel very good. I leaned against the wall to rest a moment. I looked at the breeder's pamphlet, which was still in my hand. On the back was information about how to care for the bird, and about its reproduction cycles. They emphasized the species' need to be in pairs during warm months, and the things one could do to make the years in captivity as pleasant as possible. I heard a brief shriek, and then the bathroom sink turned on. When the water started running I felt a little better, and I knew that, somehow, I would make it down the stairs.

SANTA CLAUS SLEEPS AT OUR HOUSE

The Christmas when Santa Claus spent the night at our house was the last time we were all together. Mom and Dad stopped fighting after that night, but I don't think it was because of Santa. Dad had sold his car a few months before because he'd lost his job, but he said a good Christmas tree was important that year, and he bought one even though Mom was against it. The tree came in a long, flat cardboard box, along with an instruction sheet explaining how to fit the three parts together and spread the branches open so they looked natural. Once the tree was assembled, it was taller than Dad, really huge, and I think that's one of the reasons why Santa slept at our house that year. I had asked for a remote-control car for Christmas. Any would do; I wasn't after any model in particular. The problem was that almost all the kids at school had them, and when we played at recess, the remote-control cars did nothing but crash into the regular toy cars like mine. So I had written my letter to Santa, and Dad had taken me to the post office so I could mail it. And he told the guy at the window:

"We're mailing this to Santa Claus," and he handed him the envelope.

The guy at the window didn't even greet us because there were a lot of people and you could see he was tired from so much work. The Christmas season must be the worst time of year for those guys. He took the letter, looked at it, and said:

"Zip code's missing."

"But it's for Santa Claus," said Dad, and he smiled and winked. You could see he was trying to make friends, but the guy said:

"Won't go out without a zip code."

"Now, you know Santa Claus's address doesn't have a zip code," said Dad.

"Won't go out without a zip code," said the guy, and he called the next person.

And then Dad climbed over the counter, grabbed the guy by his shirt collar, and the letter went out.

So I was worried on Christmas Eve, because I didn't know if my letter had made it to Santa or not. Plus, we hadn't been able to count on Mom for almost two months, and that had me worried, too, because the one who took care of things was always Mom, and things worked well that way. But one day she stopped caring, just like that, from one day to the next. She went to see some doctors; Dad always went with her and I stayed next door at Marcela's house. But Mom didn't get better. Then there were no more clean clothes, no more cereal and milk in the mornings. Dad dropped me off late wherever I had to go, and then he'd be late again to pick me up. When I asked for an explanation, Dad said that Mom wasn't sick and she didn't have cancer and she wasn't going to die. That something like that could very well have happened, but he wasn't such a lucky man. Marcela explained that Mom had simply stopped believing in things, and that that was called being "depressed." It made you not have any desire for anything, and it would take a while to go away. Mom didn't go to work anymore or get together with girlfriends or talk on the phone with Grandma. She just sat in her robe in front of the TV and flipped through channels all morning, all afternoon, and all night. I was in charge of feeding her. Marcela left food in the freezer with the portions labeled. I had to combine them: I couldn't, for example, give Mom all the potato casserole and then the whole vegetable tart; I had to combine the portions so her diet would be healthy. I thawed out the food in the microwave and brought it to her on a tray, with a glass of water and silverware. Mom said:

"Thank you, dear. You stay warm now." She said it without looking at me, without taking her eyes from the television.

When I got out of school it was Augusto's mother, who was beautiful, who held my hand and waited with me. That worked as long as Dad came to pick me up, but later, when Marcela started to come instead, neither of the women seemed very happy, so I waited alone under the tree on the corner. Whoever came to pick me up, they were always late.

Marcela and Dad became very good friends, and some nights Dad stayed with her next door, playing poker, and Mom and I had trouble going to sleep without him in the house. Sometimes we'd run into each other at the bathroom door and then Mom would say:

"Careful, dear, don't catch cold." And she'd go back to the TV.

Marcela spent many afternoons at our house, cooking for us and straightening up a little. I don't know why she did it. I guess Dad asked her for help and since she was his friend she felt like she had to, because the truth is she didn't look too pleased about it. A couple of times she turned off Mom's TV, sat down across from her, and said:

"Irene, we have to talk, this can't go on . . ."

She told Mom she had to change her attitude, that things couldn't go on like that, and that she, Marcela, couldn't keep doing everything. She begged Mom to react and make a decision or she'd end up ruining our lives. But Mom never answered. And finally Marcela would leave and slam the door, and that night Dad would order pizza because there was nothing for dinner, and I love pizza.

I told Augusto that Mom had stopped "believing in things," and that she was "depressed," and he wanted to see what she was like. We did something really bad that sometimes I'm ashamed of: we jumped up and down in front of her for a while, but Mom only moved her head a little when we blocked the TV. Then we made a hat out of newspaper, and we tried it out on her in different ways. We left it on her all afternoon, and she didn't even move. I took the hat off her before Dad got home. I was sure Mom wasn't going to say anything to him about it, but I felt bad anyway.

Then Christmas came. Marcela made her baked chicken with horrible vegetables, but since it was a special night she also made french fries for me. Dad asked Mom to get up off the sofa and eat with us. He carefully moved her to the table—Marcela had set it with a red tablecloth, green candles, and the plates we used when company came—sat her down at the head of the table, and took a few steps back without taking his eyes off her. I guess he thought it might work, but as soon as he was far enough away, she got up and went back to her sofa. So we moved the food out to the coffee table and we ate in there with her. The TV was on, of course, and the news had a story about a place with poor people who had received a ton of presents and food from people with more money, and so now they were really happy. I was nervous and I kept looking at the Christmas tree the whole time, because it was almost midnight and I wanted my car. Then Mom pointed at the TV. It was like seeing furniture move. Dad and Marcela looked at each other. On TV, Santa Claus was sitting in his living room, one arm hugging a boy sitting on his lap, and the other around a woman who looked like Augusto's mom. The woman leaned over and kissed Santa, and Santa looked at us and said:

". . . and when I get home, I just want to be with my family." And the logo of a coffee brand appeared on the screen.

Mom started to cry. Marcela took me by the hand and told me to go up to my room. I said no. She told me again, this time in the impatient tone she used when she talked to Mom, but nothing was going to drag me away from that tree. When Dad tried to turn the TV off, Mom started to fight with him to get him away. The doorbell rang and I said:

"It's Santa."

Marcela slapped me and then Dad yelled at her. They started to argue. And though Mom managed to turn the TV back on, Santa Claus wasn't on any of the channels.

The doorbell rang again, and Dad said:

"Who the hell is it?"

I hoped it wasn't the man from the post office, because Dad was already in a bad mood and I didn't want them to fight again.

The doorbell rang again, a bunch of times in a row, and then Dad got sick of it and went to the door, and when he opened it, I saw it *was* Santa Claus. He wasn't as fat as on TV, and he looked tired. He had trouble standing up, and he leaned for a second against one side of the doorway, then the other.

"What do you want?" asked Dad.

"I'm Santa Claus," said Santa.

"And I'm Snow White," said Dad, and slammed the door in his face.

Then Mom got up, ran to the door, and opened it. Santa was still there, trying to hold himself up, and she hugged him. Dad had a fit:

"This is the guy, Irene?" he yelled at Mom, and he started to say bad words and try to separate them. And Mom said to Santa:

"Bruno, I can't live without you, I'm dying."

Dad got them apart, and then he punched Santa and Santa fell backward and then just lay there on the stoop. Mom started screaming like crazy. I was worried about what was happening to Santa, and also because all of this was delaying the car, but I was happy to see Mom move again.

Dad told Mom he was going to kill them both, and Mom told Dad that if he was so happy with his friend Marcela, then why couldn't she be Santa's friend, which seemed logical to me. Marcela went up to Santa, who was starting to wake up on the ground, and reached out her hand to help him up. And then Dad started to say all kinds of things and Mom started to yell. Marcela was saying, "Calm down, let's go inside, please," but no one listened. Santa Claus brought his hand to the back of his neck and I saw he was bleeding. He spat at Dad and Dad said:

"You fucking fag."

And Mom said to Dad:

"You're the fag, you son of a bitch." And she spat at him, too. She gave Santa her hand, brought him into the house, led him up to her room, and closed the door.

Dad stayed there like he was frozen, and when he finally woke up, he realized I was still there, and he yelled at me to go to bed. I knew I was in no position to argue; I went to my room without Christmas and without a present. I waited in bed until everything was silent, watching the plastic fishes of my night-light swim on the wall. By then I knew I wasn't going to get my remote-control car, but Santa Claus slept at my house that night, and that meant a much better year for all of us.

THE DIGGER

I needed a rest, so I rented a big house near a coastal town far from the city. The house was ten miles from the town on a gravel road that led to the sea. The final stretch was just two dirt tracks, almost impossible to see in the tall grass; soon they disappeared entirely and I couldn't go any farther in the car. I could see the upper floor of the house in the distance, so I steeled myself to get out, take the essentials, and continue on foot. It was growing dark, and though I couldn't see the ocean, I could hear the waves crashing on the shore. I hadn't walked far when I tripped over something.

"Is that you, sir?"

I started backward.

"Sir, is that you?" A man stood up with difficulty. "I didn't waste a single day, eh . . . I swear it on my own mother . . ."

He spoke hurriedly while he smoothed the wrinkles in his clothes and arranged his hair.

"The thing is that just last night . . . You can imagine, sir, that being so close I wasn't going to leave things for the next day. Come, come," he said, and he climbed down into a hole amid the scrub, just a step away from where we were.

I knelt down and put my head in. The hole measured over a yard wide, and I couldn't make out anything inside. For whom could this worker be working, when he couldn't even recognize his own boss? What was he looking for, digging so deep?

"Sir, are you coming down?"

"I think you've made a mistake," I said.

"What?"

I told him I wasn't coming down, and, as he didn't answer, I went to the house instead. Only when I reached the front stairs did I hear a distant "Very good, sir, as you like."

The next morning, I went out to get the luggage I'd left in the car. The man was sitting on the veranda of the house, nodding off, a rusty shovel propped between his knees. When he saw me, he put the shovel down and hurried to catch up with me. He carried the heaviest luggage, and, pointing to some packages, he asked if they were part of the plan.

"I'm sorry, but I need to get organized," I said, and when we reached the door I took what he was carrying so he wouldn't come inside.

"Yes, yes, sir. As you like."

I went inside. From the kitchen windows I could see the beach. There were hardly any waves; the water was ideal for swimming. I crossed the kitchen and looked through the front window: the man was still there. He alternated between looking toward the hole and studying the sky. When I went out, he corrected his posture and greeted me respectfully.

"What are we doing, sir?"

I realized that one gesture from me would have sufficed to make the man run to the hole and start digging. I looked toward the fields, in the direction of the pit.

"How much is left, do you think?"

"Not much, sir, not much at all . . ."

"How much is not much, in your opinion?"

"Not much . . . I wouldn't know for sure."

"Do you think it's possible to finish tonight?"

"I can't promise anything . . . You know: it doesn't depend only on me."

"Well, if you want to do it so badly, do it. Finish it once and for all."

"Consider it done, sir."

I saw the man pick up the shovel, go down the stairs from the house toward the field, and disappear into the hole.

Later on I went to town. It was a sunny morning and I wanted to buy bathing trunks to take advantage of the sea; when it came down to it, I had no reason to worry about a man who was digging a hole at a house that didn't belong to me. I went into the only store I found open. When the clerk was wrapping up my purchase, he asked me:

"And how is your digger doing?"

I was silent for several seconds, maybe waiting for someone else to answer.

"My digger?"

He handed me the bag.

"Yes, your digger . . ."

I handed the man the money and looked at him, surprised. Before I left I couldn't help but ask him:

"How do you know about the digger?"

"What do you mean, how do I know about the digger?" he asked, as if he couldn't comprehend what I was saying.

I went back to the house and the digger, who was waiting asleep on the veranda, woke up as soon as I opened the door.

"Sir," he said, getting to his feet, "there's been great progress, I do believe we're getting closer and closer . . ."

"I'm going down to the beach before it gets dark."

I don't remember why it seemed like a good idea to tell him. But there he was, pleased at my comment and ready to go with me. He waited outside for me to change, and a little later we walked toward the sea.

"There's no problem with you leaving the hole?" I asked.

The digger stopped.

"Would you rather I go back?"

"No, no, I'm just asking."

"It's just that if anything happened"—he seemed poised to go back to the hole—"it would be terrible, sir."

"Terrible? What could happen?"

"Just got to keep digging."

"Why?"

He looked at the sky, first to one side, then the other.

"Well, don't worry." I went on walking. "Come with me."

The digger followed me, hesitant.

Once at the beach, a few yards from the sea, I sat down to take off my shoes and socks. The man sat next to me, put his shovel aside, and took off his boots.

"Do you know how to swim?" I asked. "Why don't you come in with me?"

"No, sir. I'll just watch, if you don't mind. And I brought the shovel, in case you come up with a new plan."

I stood up and walked toward the sea. The water was cold, but I knew the man was watching me and I didn't want to back out.

When I returned, the digger wasn't there.

With a doomed feeling, I looked for footprints heading

toward the water in case he had followed my suggestion, but I didn't see anything and I decided to go back. I looked in and around the hole. In the house, I made an uneasy tour of the rooms. I stopped on the landings of the stairs and I called to him from the hallways, a bit embarrassed. Later, I went outside again. I walked to the hole, looked in, and called to him again. I couldn't see anything. I lay facedown on the ground, stuck my hand in, and felt the walls: this was a meticulous job. The hole was approximately three feet wide and seemed to go down toward the center of the earth. I entertained the possibility of getting in, but right away I ruled it out. When I put one hand on the ground to push myself up, the edge crumbled. I held on to the scrub, and, paralyzed, I heard the sound of the earth falling in the darkness. My knees slipped on the edge and I saw the mouth of the hole break apart and disappear inside it. I stood up and observed the disaster. I looked fearfully around me, but I didn't see the digger anywhere. Then it occurred to me that I could fix the edges with a little damp earth, although I would need a shovel and some water.

I went back to the house. I opened the closets, went through two back rooms that I was entering for the first time, and searched the laundry room. Finally, in a box with other old tools, I found a trowel. It was small, but it would be a start. When I went out of the house, I found myself face-to-face with the digger. I hid the trowel behind my back.

"I was looking for you, sir. We have a problem."

For the first time, the digger was looking at me with distrust.

"What is it?" I asked.

"Someone else has been digging."

"Someone else? Are you sure?"

"I know the job. Someone has been digging."

"And where were you?"

"I was sharpening my shovel."

"Okay," I said, trying to be decisive. "You dig as much as you can and don't wander off again. I'll keep an eye on the surroundings."

He hesitated. He took a few steps away but then stopped and turned back toward me. Distracted, I had let my arm fall and the trowel hung alongside my legs.

"Are you going to dig, sir?" He looked at me.

Instinctively, I hid the shovel. He seemed not to recognize in me the man I had been for him up until a moment before.

"Are you going to dig?" he repeated.

"I'll help you. You dig for a while and I'll take over when you're tired."

"The hole is yours," he said. "You can't dig."

Then the digger lifted up his shovel and, looking me in the eyes, drove it into the ground again.

IRMAN

Oliver was driving. I was so thirsty I was starting to feel dizzy. The truck stop we found was empty. The restaurant was big, like everything else out in the country, and the tables were littered with crumbs and bottles, as if a battalion had just eaten lunch and there hadn't been time to clean up. We chose a spot by the window, near a whirring fan that didn't move a hair on our heads. I desperately needed to drink something, and I said so to

Oliver. He grabbed a menu from another table and started reading aloud the options he found interesting.

A man appeared from behind the plastic curtain. He was extremely short. He had an apron tied around his waist and a grimy kitchen rag draped over his arm. Although he seemed to be the waiter, he looked disoriented, as if someone had plopped him down there all of a sudden and he didn't really know what he was supposed to do next. He walked over to us. We said hello; he nodded. Oliver ordered the drinks and made a joke about the heat, but he couldn't get the guy to open his mouth. I got the feeling we'd be doing him a favor if we kept our order simple, so I asked if there was a daily special, something fresh and quick, and he said yes and walked away, as though *something fresh and quick* were an option on the menu and there was nothing more to say.

He went back to the kitchen, and we saw his head bobbing up and down in the window above the counter as his small figure passed by. I looked at Oliver and he was smiling; I was too thirsty to laugh. Some time passed, much longer than it should take to choose two cold bottles of whatever and bring them to the table, and finally the man appeared again. He wasn't carrying anything, not even an empty glass. I felt awful. I thought that if I didn't drink something right away I was going to go crazy. What was wrong with this guy, anyway? What question could he have? He stopped at the table. There were drops of sweat on his forehead, and his shirt was stained under his arms.

He made a confused motion with his hand as if he was going to give some kind of explanation, but then stopped short.

I asked what was going on, I guess in a somewhat violent tone. He turned back toward the kitchen, and then, shuffling, he said:

"It's just, I can't reach the fridge."

I looked over at Oliver. Oliver couldn't hold back his laughter, and that put me in an even worse mood.

"What do you mean, you can't reach the fridge? How the hell do you wait on customers?"

"It's just . . ." He wiped his forehead with the rag. The guy was a disaster. "My wife is the one who gets things from the fridge," he said.

"And . . . ?" I felt like punching him.

"She's on the floor. She fell and she's—"

"What do you mean, 'on the floor'?" interrupted Oliver.

"Well, I don't know. I don't know . . ." he repeated, shrugging his shoulders, the palms of his hands turned upward.

"Where is she?" asked Oliver.

The guy pointed to the kitchen. The only thing I wanted was to drink something cool, and when I saw Oliver stand up, all my hopes were dashed.

"Where?" Oliver asked again.

The guy pointed to the kitchen once more and Oliver moved off in that direction, turning back to look at us a few times, as though distrustful. It was strange when he disappeared behind the curtain and left me alone, face-to-face, with an idiot like that.

I had to sidestep around him when Oliver called me into the kitchen. I walked slowly because I could tell something was wrong. I opened the curtain and peeked in. The kitchen was small and overflowing with casserole dishes, saucepans, plates, and things piled up on shelves or hanging from hooks.

Lying on the floor a few feet from the wall, the woman looked like a marine beast washed up by the tide. She was huge, and she clutched a big plastic spoon in her left hand. The fridge hung above her, flush with the cupboards. It was one of those kiosk refrigerators with a transparent lid, the kind that stands on the floor and slides open on top, only this one had ridiculously been tacked to the wall with brackets, following the line of the cupboards, its doors facing outward. Oliver was looking at me.

"Well," I told him, "you came back here, now do something."

I heard the plastic curtain move, and the man came and stood next to me. He was much shorter than he'd looked before, now that we were both standing. I think I had almost three heads on him. Oliver knelt down next to the fat woman, but couldn't seem to bring himself to touch her. I thought she could wake up at any moment and start shouting. He brushed the hair from her face. Her eyes were closed.

"Help me turn her over," said Oliver.

The guy didn't even blink. I went over and knelt down on

the other side, but between the two of us, we could barely move her.

"Aren't you going to help?" I asked the man.

"I'm . . . ahhh . . . suspect . . ." babbled the moron, "she's dead."

We immediately let go of the fat woman and sat there looking at her.

"What do you mean, dead? Why didn't you say she was dead?"

"I'm not sure, it's just a suspicion."

"He said he's a suspect," said Oliver, "not that he suspects."

"I also suspect my suspicion."

Oliver looked at me; his face was saying something like *Any second now I'll beat the shit out of this guy.*

I lifted the hand with the spoon to check for a pulse. When Oliver got tired of waiting for me, he put two fingers under the woman's nose and mouth and said:

"She's a goner. Let's get out of here."

And then the damned little guy got desperate.

"What do you mean, 'get out of here'? No, please. I can't deal with her alone."

Oliver opened the fridge, took out two sodas and handed one to me, and took a few steps away, cursing. I followed him. I opened my bottle and I thought its mouth would never meet mine. I had forgotten how thirsty I was.

"So? What do you think?" asked Oliver. I breathed in relief.

Suddenly I felt ten years younger and in a better mood. "Did she fall or did he take her out?" he asked. We were still pretty close to the short guy and Oliver didn't lower his voice.

"I don't think it was him," I said in a low voice. "He needs her to reach the fridge, doesn't he?"

"He could reach . . ."

"You really think he killed her?"

"He could use a ladder, get up on the table, he's got fifty bar stools . . ." he said, motioning around us. It seemed to me he was talking loudly on purpose, so I lowered my voice even more:

"Maybe he really is just a poor guy. Maybe he really is that stupid, and now he's all alone with his fat wife dead in the kitchen."

"You want to adopt him? Put him in the back of the truck and set him free when we get there?"

I took a few more sips. The idiot was standing over the fat woman and holding a stool in the air, seeming not to know where to put it. Oliver signaled to me, and we left the kitchen. In the dining room, we went behind the counter, and, through the window that looked into the kitchen, we watched him put the stool aside, take hold of the fat woman's arm, and start to pull. He couldn't move her an inch. He rested a few seconds and pulled again. He tried putting the chair over her, one of its legs against her knee. He clambered up on it and reached as far as he could toward the fridge, but now that he had the height, the stool was too far away. When he turned toward us to get down, we ducked and hid, sitting on the floor with our backs to the wall. I was surprised to see there was nothing under the counter. There were things up on the shelves, and above those, the cupboards and racks were also full, but there was nothing down at our level. We heard him move the stool. Sigh. There was silence and we waited. Suddenly he burst out from behind the curtain brandishing a knife. He saw us sitting on the floor, and far from being annoyed, he breathed in relief.

"I can't reach the fridge," he said.

We didn't even stand up.

"You can't reach anything," said Oliver.

The guy stood looking at Oliver as if God himself had come down to earth and told him the meaning of life. He dropped the knife and his eyes took in the empty expanse under the counter. Oliver was satisfied: the guy seemed to go beyond any horizon of stupidity.

"Let's see, make us an omelet," said Oliver.

The man turned back toward the kitchen. His imbecilic face took in the utensils, the casserole dishes, almost the entire kitchen hanging from the walls or the shelves. He looked astonished.

"Okay, so not that," said Oliver. "Make some simple sandwiches, surely you can do that."

"No," said the guy. "I can't reach the sandwich maker."

"Don't toast it. Just bring ham, cheese, and some bread."

"No," he said. "No." He shook his head; he seemed ashamed.

"Okay. A glass of water, then."

He shook his head again.

"How the hell did you serve this army?" asked Oliver, indicating the dirty tables.

"I need to think."

"You don't need to think, what you need is a few feet more."

"I can't do it without her . . ."

I thought about getting down a cool drink for him, I thought it could do him good, but when I started to get up Oliver stopped me.

"He has to do it on his own," he said. "He has to learn."

"Oliver . . ."

"Tell me something that you can do, one thing, anything."

"I carry the food she gives me, I clean the tables . . ."

"Doesn't look like it," said Oliver.

". . . I can mix the salads and season them if she leaves everything for me on the counter. I wash the dishes, clean the floor, shake out the—"

"Okay, okay. I get it."

Then the guy stood looking at Oliver, as if surprised:

"You . . ." he said. "You can reach the fridge. You could cook, hand me things . . ."

"Say what? No one's handing you anything."

"But you could work, you're tall enough." He took a shy step toward Oliver, which to me didn't seem very wise. "I'd pay you," he said.

Oliver turned to me. "This guy's fucking with me, he's fucking with me."

"I have money. Four hundred a week? I can pay you. Five hundred?"

"You pay five hundred a week? Why don't you have a palace in the backyard? This asshole . . ."

I got up and stood behind Oliver: he was going to throw a punch any second. I think the only thing stopping him was the guy's height.

We saw the guy close his little fists as though squeezing an invisible mass between his fingers, compressing it smaller and smaller. His arms started to tremble, and he turned purple.

"My money is none of your business," he said.

Oliver kept looking at me every time the other man spoke to him, as if he couldn't believe what he was hearing. He almost seemed to be enjoying it, but I know him better than anyone: no one tells Oliver what to do.

"And judging by the truck you drive," said the guy as he looked out toward the road, "judging by your truck, one might say I manage money better than you."

"Son of a bitch," said Oliver, and he lunged at the guy. I managed to restrain him. The guy took a step back, without fear and with a dignity that added a few feet to his height. He waited until Oliver was calm and I'd let go of him.

"Okay," said Oliver. "Okay."

He stood looking at the guy; he was furious, but there was something else underneath his composure. Then he said:

"Where's the money?"

I looked at Oliver without understanding.

"Are you going to rob me?"

"I'm going to do whatever the fuck I feel like, you piece of shit."

"What are you doing?" I asked.

Oliver took a step, grabbed the guy by the front of his shirt, and lifted him into the air.

"Where's your money? Let's have it."

The force with which Oliver had lifted him up left him swinging a little side to side. But the guy looked Oliver directly in the eyes and didn't open his mouth.

Oliver let go of him. The guy fell, then adjusted his shirt.

"Okay," said Oliver. "Either you bring the money or I'll break your face."

He raised a tightly closed fist and held it an inch away from the guy's nose.

"All right," said the short man; he took a slow step back, crossed the bar in the opposite direction from the kitchen, and disappeared through a door.

"Piece of shit."

I moved closer to Oliver so the guy couldn't hear us.

"What are you doing? He's got his wife dead in the kitchen, let's go."

"Did you hear what he said about my truck? The asshole wants to hire me. He wants to be my boss, get it?"

Oliver started looking over the shelves above the bar, rifling through bottles, boxes, papers.

"The fucker's money must be around here somewhere."

"Oliver, let's go. You're crazy."

He picked up a wooden box. It was old and had the word "Habanos" hand-carved on the lid.

"Here we are," said Oliver.

"Get out of here right now," we heard a voice say.

The short guy was standing in the middle of the room, and he was holding a double-barreled shotgun aimed right at Oliver's head. Oliver hid the box behind his back. The guy clicked off the gun's safety and said:

"One."

"We're going," I said, and I took Oliver by the arm and started to walk. "I'm sorry, I'm really sorry. And I'm sorry about your wife, too, I . . ."

I had to use all my strength to get Oliver to follow me, the way mothers pull on stubborn children.

"Two."

We passed right by him, the shotgun a couple feet from Oliver's head.

"I'm sorry," I said again.

We were close to the door. I let Oliver go out first so the guy wouldn't see that he was carrying the box.

"Three."

I let go of Oliver and ran to the truck. I don't know if Oliver was afraid or not, but he didn't run. I had to wait a few seconds clutching the handle of my door for him to open it. He put the box on the seat, started the engine, and we went out the same way we'd come in. The truck bumped a few times over the curb and then we were finally on the road. Only a while later, without taking his eyes from the highway, did he say:

"Open it."

"We should . . ."

"Open it, you faggot."

I picked up the box. It was light and too small to contain a fortune. It had a fake lock, like a toy treasure chest. I opened it.

"What's in it? How much? How much?"

"You just drive," I said. "I think it's only papers."

Oliver turned every once in a while to look at what I'd found. There was a name embossed on the underside of the lid; it said "Irman," and beneath it was a photo of the short guy when he was very young, sitting on some suitcases in a terminal. He looked happy. I wondered who had taken the photo. There were also letters headed with his name: *Dear Irman*; *Irman, my love*; poems he had signed; a mint candy turned to dust; and a plastic medal for the best poet of the year with the logo of a social club.

"Is there money or not?"

"They're letters," I said.

Oliver grabbed the box from my hands and tossed it out the window.

"What are you doing?" I turned around a second to see the things scattered over the asphalt, the papers still in the air, the medal bouncing farther away.

"They're letters," he said.

And a while later:

"Look . . . We should have stopped here. 'All-you-can-eat barbecue,' did you see the sign? How much was it?"

And he shifted restlessly in his seat, as though he really did regret it.

THE TEST

The Mole says, *Name,* and I answer. I'd waited for him where I'd been told to and he came to pick me up in the Peugeot that I'm driving now. We've just met. He doesn't look at me—they say he never looks anyone in the eyes. *Age,* he says. Forty-two, I say, and when he says, *You're old,* I think that he must be older. He wears a pair of small dark glasses, and that must be why he's called the Mole. He orders me to drive to the nearest plaza and then settles into his seat, relaxed. The test is easy but it's very important to pass it, and so I'm nervous. If I don't do things right, I won't get in, and if I don't get in, there's no money. Money's the only reason to get in.

Beating a dog to death in the Buenos Aires port is the test they use to see if you're capable of doing something worse. They say, *Something worse,* and then look away, dissembling, as if we, those on the outside, didn't know that *worse* means killing a person, beating a person to death.

When the avenue splits into two streets, I opt for the quieter one. A line of red lights changes to green, one after another, and lets us speed ahead until a space, dark and green, appears between the buildings. It occurs to me that it's possible there are no dogs in this plaza, and then the Mole orders me to stop. *You didn't bring a club,* he says. No, I say. *But you're not going to beat a dog to death without a weapon.* I look at him but don't answer. I know he's going to say something, because I know him now; it's easy to figure him out. But he enjoys the silence, enjoys thinking that every word he says is a strike against me. Then he swallows and seems to think: *You won't be killing anyone.* And finally he says: *I happen to have a shovel in the trunk, you can use that.* And I'm sure that beneath his sunglasses, his eyes are shining with pleasure.

There are several dogs sleeping near the central fountain. The shovel firm in my hands—my chance could come any second— I approach. Some of them start to wake up. They yawn, stand up, look at one another, look at me; they growl, and as I get closer they shrink back. To kill someone in particular, someone already chosen, is easy. But to choose the one who will die requires time and experience. The oldest dog or the prettiest or the one that seems most aggressive. I have to choose. I'm sure the Mole is watching from the car and smiling. He must think anyone who's not like them is incapable of killing.

The dogs surround and sniff me, and some move farther away and lie back down, forgetting me. To the Mole, behind the dark glass of the car and his darkened glasses, I must be small and ridiculous, clutching the shovel and surrounded by dogs that now drift back to sleep. A white spotted one growls at a black one, and when the black one snaps at it, a third dog comes over, barks, and bares its teeth. Then the first dog bites the black one and the black one, teeth shining in the night, takes it by the neck and shakes it. I raise the shovel and the blow hits the spotted dog's back; howling, he falls. He lies still. I think it'll be easy to move him, but when I grab him by the legs he reacts and bites my arm and the blood gushes out. I raise the shovel again and hit him in the head. The dog falls back down and looks up at me from the ground, breathing fast but not moving.

Slowly at first, then more confidently, I gather his legs together, pick him up and carry him to the car. A shadow moves in the trees. A drunk peers out and says, "You just don't do that. The dogs will remember you, and later they'll take their revenge. They know," he says, "they know. Understand?" And he sits down on a bench and looks at me nervously. When I'm about to reach the car I see the Mole sitting and waiting for me in the same position he was in before, but the trunk of the Peugeot is open. The dog falls like dead weight, and he looks up at me as I close the trunk. Once I'm in the car, the Mole says: *If you'd put it on the ground it would have gotten up and run away.* Yes, I say. *No,* he says, *you should have opened the trunk first.* Yes, I say. *No, you should have done it and you didn't do it,* he says. Yes, I say, and regret it immediately, but the Mole doesn't say anything, and he looks at my hands. I look at my hands, I look at the steering wheel, and I see that everything is bloodstained, there's blood on my pants and on the floor of the car. *You should have used gloves,* he says. The wound hurts. *The man comes to kill a dog and he doesn't bring gloves,* he says. Yes, I say. *No,* he says. I know, I say, and then I shut up. I decide not to mention the pain. I start the car and drive smoothly off.

I try to concentrate, to figure out which of the many streets I pass could take me to the port without the Mole having to tell me anything. I can't afford to make another mistake. Maybe it would be good to stop at a pharmacy and buy a pair of gloves, but pharmacy gloves wouldn't work and the hardware stores will be closed by now. A plastic bag is no good, either. I could take off my jacket, roll it around my hand and use it as a glove. Yes, that's how I'm going to do the job. I think about that: the job. I'm pleased to think I can talk like they do. I take Caseros Street, which I think goes down to the port. The Mole doesn't look at me, doesn't talk to me, doesn't move; he keeps his eyes straight ahead and his breathing under control. I think they call him the Mole because his eyes under those glasses are tiny.

After several blocks Caseros crosses Chacabuco. Then Brasil, which leads to the port. I turn abruptly and the car tips onto two wheels. In the trunk the body thumps and then there are noises, as if the dog were still trying to get up. The Mole, I think surprised by the animal's strength, smiles and points to the right. I turn onto Brasil braking; the tires squeal, and with the car on two wheels again, there's more noise from the trunk—the dog scrambling to avoid the shovel and all the other stuff that's back there. The Mole says, *Brake*, and I brake. He says: *Speed up*. He smiles. I speed up. *Faster*, he says, and I go faster. Then he says, *Brake*, and I brake. Now that the dog has been thrown around several times, the Mole relaxes and says: *Keep going*. He doesn't say anything else. I drive. The street I'm driving on has no more stoplights or white lines, and the buildings get older and older. Any moment now we'll be at the port.

The Mole signals to the right. He tells me to go three more blocks and turn left, toward the water. I obey. Soon we reach the port and I stop the car in a parking lot full of stacked containers. I look at the Mole, but he doesn't look at me. Without wasting any time, I get out of the car and open the trunk. I didn't wrap the jacket around my arm but I don't need gloves anymore; the thing is done. I just need to finish quickly so we can go. In the empty port there are only a few weak yellow lights in the distance that illuminate a few ships. Maybe the dog is already dead. I think how that would have been for the best, that I should have hit him harder the first time and then he would surely be dead by now. Less work, less time with the Mole. I would have killed the dog right away, but this is how the Mole does things. It's a whim. Bringing the dog half dead to the port doesn't make anyone braver. Killing him in front of all those other dogs would have been harder.

When I touch him, when I grab his feet to take him out of the car, he opens his eyes and looks at me. I let go and he falls back into the trunk. With one front paw he scratches the rug that's now covered in blood; he tries to get up and the back part of his body is trembling. He's still breathing, and his breath is agitated. The Mole is probably timing me. I pick the dog up again and something must hurt because he howls, though he's no longer struggling. I put him on the ground and drag him away from the car. When I turn back to the trunk to get the shovel, the Mole gets out. Now he's next to the dog, looking down at him. I carry the shovel over, I see the Mole's back and beyond him, on the ground, the dog. If no one will find out about a dead dog, no one will know anything that happens here. The Mole doesn't turn around when he tells me: *Now*. I raise the shovel. *Now*, I think. But I don't bring it down. *Now*, says the Mole.

I don't bring it down, not on the Mole's back or on the dog. *Now*, he says, and then the shovel slices through the air and hits the dog's head, and the dog howls, trembles a moment, and then everything is quiet.

I start the car. Now the Mole is going to tell me who I'll work for, what my name will be, and how much money I'll make, which is what matters. *Take Huergo and then turn onto Carlos Calvo,* he says.

I've been driving for a while now. The Mole says: *At the next street, stop on the right.* I obey, and then the Mole looks at me for the first time. *Get out,* he says. I get out and he moves into the driver's seat. I peer in through the window and ask him what will happen now. *Nothing,* he says, *you hesitated.* He starts the car and the Peugeot moves off in silence. When I look around I realize he left me in the plaza. The same plaza. In the center, near the fountain, a pack of dogs gets up, slowly, and looks at me.

TOWARD HAPPY CIVILIZATION

He's lost his ticket, and from behind the ticket window's white bars, the station agent refuses to sell him another, saying there's no change in the drawer. From a station bench, he looks at the immense, dry countryside that opens out in all directions. He crosses his legs and unfolds the pages of the newspaper in search of articles that will make the time pass faster. Night spreads across the sky, and far away, above the black line beyond which the tracks disappear, a yellow light announces the next train.

Gruner stands up. The newspaper hangs from his hand like an obsolete weapon. In the ticket window he discerns a smile that, half hidden behind the bars, is directed exclusively at him. A skinny dog that was sleeping now stands up, attentive. Gruner moves toward the window, confident in the hospitality of country people, in masculine camaraderie, in the goodwill that awakens in men when you handle them well. He is going to say, *Please, how hard can it be? You know there's no more time to find change.* And if the man refuses, he's going to ask about other options: *Surely, sir, I could buy the ticket aboard the train, or, when I arrive, I could buy it at the terminal's ticket office. Make me an IOU, give me a piece of paper that says I have to pay for the ticket later.*

But when he reaches the window, when the train's lights lengthen the shadows and the whistle is loud and intrusive, Gruner discovers that no one is there behind the bars, there's only a tall chair and a table overflowing with unstamped slips, future tickets to various destinations. As he watches the train barrel into the station, Gruner also sees that off to one side of the tracks, in the field, the still-smiling man is signaling to the conductor that he doesn't have to stop, since no one has bought a ticket. Then, as the sound of the massive machine moves away, the dog lies down again and the station's only lamp blinks for a few seconds, then goes out entirely. The now crumpled newspaper comes to rest again on Gruner's lap, and he reaches no conclusion that would send him off in search of that wretch who has refused him the capital's happy civilization.

Everything is still and silent. Even Gruner, sitting at one end of a bench with the cool night seeping in through his clothes, stays motionless and breathes calmly. A shadow that he doesn't see moves between posts and plaza benches and reveals itself as the man from the ticket window. Now unsmiling, he sits at the other end of the bench and puts a mug full of steaming liquid down next to him. He pushes it until it's a few inches from Gruner. He clears his throat and looks at the wide black countryside that stretches out before them. As the steam from the mug awakens Gruner's appetite, he focuses on resistance. He thinks that in the end, he will get to the capital somehow and he'll report what has happened. But his hand moves toward the mug of its own accord, and the heat between his fingers distracts him. "There's more where that came from," says the man, and then Gruner—but no, Gruner wouldn't have done that. Gruner's hands take the warm vessel and raise it to his mouth, where a miraculous medicine reanimates his body. With the last sip he understands that, if this were a war, that wretch would already have won two battles. Victorious, the man stands, picks up the empty mug, and walks away.

The dog is still curled up, its snout hidden between its stomach and hind legs, and although Gruner has called to him several times, the dog ignores him. It occurs to Gruner that it was the dog's food in the mug, and he worriedly wonders how long that dog has been here. Whether there had been a time when the dog had also wanted to travel from one place to another, as he

himself had wanted to do that very afternoon. He has the notion
that the dogs of the world are the result of men who have failed
in their attempted journeys. Men nourished and retained with
nothing but steaming broth, men whose hair grows long and
whose ears droop and whose tails lengthen, a feeling of terror
and cold inciting them to stay silent, curled up under some train-
station bench, contemplating the failures of the newcomer who
is just like them only still has hope, staunchly awaiting the opportunity of a voyage.

A silhouette moves in the ticket office. Gruner stands up and
walks decisively over. Steam from the heaters wafts out between
the white bars, carrying homey smells. The man smiles with
goodwill and offers him more broth. Gruner asks what time the
next train passes. "In an hour," says the man, and his offended
hand shuts the ticket window and leaves Gruner alone once again.

Everything repeats like in a natural cycle, thinks Gruner an
hour later, as he forlornly watches another string of cars go by
without stopping, an exact copy of the previous train. In any
case, morning will come soon and workers will arrive at the station to buy tickets, many of them probably with change. If there
are trains to the capital, it is thanks to the passengers who must
travel there every morning. *Yes, as soon as I get to the capital I
will report that man*, thinks Gruner, *and someday I'll come back
with change to this wretch's station just to make sure he no longer
works here*. With the relief of that certainty, he sits on the bench
and waits.

Time passes, during which Gruner's eyes get used to the night and read shapes in even the darkest places. That's how he discovers the woman, her figure leaning against the waiting-room doorway, and he sees her hand waving to invite him in. Gruner is sure that the gesture was for him, and he stands up and walks toward her; she smiles and ushers him in.

On the table are three plates, all of them served, and the steam comes not from soup, broth, or dog food, but from substantial sausages bathed in an aromatic white cream. The room smells like chicken, cheese, and potatoes, and then, when the woman brings a casserole dish full of vegetables to the table, Gruner remembers the dinners typical of the capital's happy civilization. The miserable ticket man, so elusive when it came to buying a ticket, enters and offers Gruner a seat.

"Have a seat, please. Make yourself at home."

The man and woman begin to eat, satisfied. Gruner sits with them, his plate also heaped with food. He knows that, outside, the cold is damp and inhospitable, and he also knows he has lost another battle, since he wastes no time in raising the first forkful of an exquisite chicken sausage to his mouth. But the food doesn't guarantee he'll get out of this station soon.

"Is there a reason you won't sell me a ticket?" asks Gruner.

The man looks at the woman and asks for dessert. From the oven emerges an apple tart that is soon cut into equal slices. The man and woman exchange a tender glance when they see how Gruner devours his portion.

"Pe, show him his room, he must be tired," says the woman, and then the first mouthful of a second serving of tart stops en route to Gruner's mouth, stops and waits.

Pe stands up and asks Gruner to come with him.

"You can sleep inside. It's cold out there. There are no more trains until morning."

I have no choice, thinks Gruner, and he leaves the tart and follows the man to the guest room.

"Your room," says the man.

I'm not going to pay for this, thinks Gruner, at the same time as he sees that the two blankets on the bed look new and warm. He's still going to lodge a complaint; the hospitality doesn't make up for what happened. The couple's conversation reaches him faintly from the room next door. Before he drifts off, Gruner hears the woman tell Pe that he needs to be more considerate, the man is alone and this must seem strange, and Pe's offended voice replies that the only thing that wretch cares about is buying his return ticket. "Ungrateful" is the last thing that reaches his ears; the sound of the word fades gradually and is reborn in the morning, when the whistle of a train already passing the station wakes him up to a new day in the country.

"We didn't wake you because you were sleeping so soundly," says the woman. "I hope you don't mind."

Hot coffee with milk and cinnamon toast with butter and honey. While Gruner eats breakfast in silence, his eyes follow the woman's steps as she cooks what will apparently be lunch.

Then something happens. An office worker, a man with Asian features and dressed like Gruner, someone who is possibly taking the next train and has enough change for two tickets, comes into the kitchen and greets the woman.

"Morning, Fi," he says, and with a son's affection he kisses the woman on the cheek. "I'm finished outside. Should I help Pe in the field?"

Once again, the food that was moving toward Gruner's mouth, in this case a piece of toast, stops halfway and hangs in the air.

"No, Cho, thanks," says Fi. "Gong and Gill already went, and three are enough for the job. Could you get a rabbit for supper?"

"Sure," replies Cho, and with apparent enthusiasm he takes down the rifle hanging next to the chimney and withdraws.

Gruner's toast returns to the plate and stays there. Gruner is going to ask something but then the door opens, and in comes Cho again. He looks first at Gruner and then curiously asks the woman:

"Is he new?"

Fi smiles and looks affectionately at Gruner.

"He got here yesterday.

Gruner's actions that first day are the same as those of everyone who has ever been in his situation. Hide away offended and spend the morning next to the office that sells tickets for a train that doesn't come. Then, refuse to eat lunch, and in the afternoon, secretly study the group's activities. Under Pe's instructions, the office workers work the earth. Barefoot, their pants rolled up to the ankles, they smile and laugh at their own jokes without losing the rhythm of their tasks. Then Fi brings tea for them all, and the four of them—Pe, Cho, Gong, and Gill—signal to Gruner, who thought he was hidden, inviting him to join the group.

But Gruner, as we know, refuses. There's no one more stubborn than an office worker like him. Held over from offices with no partitions, but with a telephone line all his own, he still has his pride when he's out in the country, and sitting on a wooden bench, he struggles not to move all afternoon long. *Even if no train comes*, he thinks. *Even if I rot right here.*

The night gathers everyone together in the preparation of a warm family meal, as the lights of the house turn on one by one and the first aromas of what will be a great feast escape into the cold through the cracks under the doors. Gruner, his patience and pride attenuated by the passage of the day, gives up guiltlessly and accepts the invitation: a door that opens and the woman who, as on the previous night, invites him in. Inside, a familial murmur. Pe congratulates the office workers with brotherly slaps on the back. The workers, grateful for everything, set a table that reminds Gruner of the intimate Christmas celebrations of his childhood, and—why not?—of the capital's happy civilization. A triumphant Cho—successful, satisfied hunter—serves up the rabbit. Pe and Fi sit at either end of the rectangular table. On one side are the office workers, and all alone across from them sits Gruner. At Gong's and Gill's constant requests he passes a saltshaker back and forth, though it is never actually used. Finally, Pe discovers eager smiles tinged with mischief on Gong's and Gill's childish faces, and with a call to attention he frees Gruner from the exhausting game so he can finally taste his first mouthful of the meal.

Over the following days Gruner tries out various strategies. The first thing that occurs to him is to bribe Pe, or even Fi, for change. Then, with tears in his eyes, he offers to buy the ticket to the city in exchange for all his money: "No change," he begs, "keep it all," he begs over and over again. And he listens desperately to a reply that speaks of a certain railroad code of ethics and the impossibility of keeping someone else's money. Those are the days Gruner proposes to buy something from them. The amount of the ticket plus anything they want to sell him will be the sum total of his money—the perfect bargain. But no. And he has to bear the office workers' stifled laughter, and then another family dinner.

The first of Gruner's tasks to become routine are washing the dishes after dinner and, in the morning, preparing the dog's food. Then he begs again. He offers to pay with his work. To pay for something, pay for lunch. Chip in little by little with the work of living in the country. Chat every now and then with the office workers. Discover incredible talents in Gong when it comes to theories of efficiency and group work. In Gill, a lawyer of great prestige. In Cho, a capable accountant. Cry once again in front of the ticket office, and at night offer to make lunch the next day. Hunt field rabbits with Cho, and suggest, in thanks for the family's goodwill, compensating them at least for the delicious food. Learn how this is done, and how one should do that, and also try to pay for that all-important information, that the harvest is done in the morning when the sun won't bother you, and the midday hours are spent on housework. And every once in a while, with the hope of getting change for a ticket—a hope that is reborn only on certain days—sit on the station bench and watch another train that, at Pe's inevitable signals, passes without stopping.

Then, bit by bit, begin to see the office workers' happiness as false. Doubt it all: Cho's innocent gratitude, Gong's spirited hospitality, and Gill's unflaggingly subservient attitude. Intuit in all their actions a secret plan that goes against the love that Pe and Fi profess for them. And then something happens. It's a thing that he no longer expects, and it takes him by surprise. It starts with an invitation: Cho, Gong, and Gill will make Mother and Father's bed. Gruner is invited. They go into the master bedroom and, as a team, spread out the sheets and smooth the creases. And that's how it happens that something is revealed: Gong smiles and looks at Gill, and together, facing each other on either side of the bed, they each lift up a pillow, and before the surprised eyes of Gruner and Cho, spit onto the sheets before setting them down again.

It's the moment they're rebelling and Gruner knows it—so

much love couldn't have been real. So he gathers his courage. Gruner asks:

"Do any of you have change?"

All three seem surprised. Maybe it's still too soon for the question, but then so, too, for the answer:

"Do you?"

Gruner says:

"Do you think I'd be here if I did?"

And they:

"Would *we*?"

During a long silence, they all seem to draw conclusions that merge, and start to formulate a plan that, though still undefined, now unites them in a newfound but sincere kinship. As if the action could hide the words they'd uttered, Gill shyly straightens the sheets on a bed that is already smooth. And that night, when the euphoric familial love is reborn, Gruner understands that it has always been part of a farce that began many years before he arrived. And now nothing keeps him from enjoying Pe's educational advice or the tender kisses Fi plants on her men's foreheads when they say good night and go to bed. In the morning he submits gladly to the routine, everyday activity, and at night, when doubt invades him and he starts to think maybe his bold plan is born of his own self-delusion, he realizes that the noises bothering him are really the light little taps of someone knocking at his door. Taps that, like passwords to be deciphered, invite him to get up and open the door, to find an anxious Cho standing there. Under orders from Gong, he's come to bring Gruner to their first meeting.

The gathering is in the public bathrooms next to the ticket window. Gill, ever efficient, has covered the broken windows with cardboard so the cold doesn't seep in, and he's brought candles and snacks. Everything is set out on a tablecloth spread neatly over the floor in the middle of the bathroom. Sitting cross-legged, attentive like true office workers, the four of them settle around the tablecloth and pool their money in Gong's hand. Four bills, large and crisp. It's strange for Gruner to discover a new expression on his companions' childlike faces, a mixture of anxiety and distrust. Maybe it's been months, maybe years, they've been here; maybe they suspect that they've lost everything back in the capital. Wives, children, jobs, homes, everything they had before they got stranded here in this station. Gill's eyes grow damp, and a tear falls onto the tablecloth. Cho pats Gill on the back a few times and lets him lean his head on his shoulder. Then Gong looks at Gruner; they know Gill and Cho are weak, that they're worn-out and they no longer believe in the possibility of escape, only in the pitiful consolation of more days in the country. Gong and Gruner, who are strong, will have to fight for all four of them. An unsparing plan, thinks Gruner, and in Gong's eyes he finds an ally who follows every one of his thoughts with attention. Gill goes on crying, and he wails:

"With all this money we could buy part of the land, we could at least live independently . . ."

"The train has to stop," resolves Gong, with a seriousness he hasn't shown before.

"What do you want to do?" asks Gruner. "How do you stop a train? We have to be realistic here, objectivity is the foundation of any good plan."

"Tell us, Gruner—why do you think the train doesn't stop?" asks Gong.

And Cho replies anxiously:

"It's because of Pe, he signals that there are no passengers."

"We know the signal for 'Don't stop.' What we don't know is the signal for 'Do stop,'" says Gong.

"I see," says Gruner. And then, illuminated: "And did you already try the negative?"

"The negative?" asks Gong.

"If 'the signal' means 'Don't stop,'" says Gruner, "'the negative' is . . ."

"No signal!" cries Cho.

"We'll have to pray," says Gruner.

"We'll have to pray," repeats Gill, wiping his eyes with a paper napkin.

It all happens just as it should, as they'd set out in the plan. First of all, dawn breaks. Fi pokes her head through the kitchen door and calls the family to breakfast. The little office workers, each one in his own room, put socks on their feet, jackets over their pajamas, slippers on their stockinged feet. Pe is the first to use the bathroom, and the others follow in order of their arrival: Gong, Gill, Cho, and finally Gruner, who, since he knows he's last, uses the time to feed the dog, by that time already waiting by the door. Fi greets them all and hurries them along so breakfast doesn't get cold. Then Cho distracts Fi, bringing her over to the window and pointing to something in the fields, maybe an animal that could be that day's lunch or dinner. Meanwhile, Gong watches the bathroom door to be sure Pe doesn't come out; after all, he is next in line and it's not strange for him to wait outside. And that's when Gruner and Gill dissolve the sleeping pills stolen from Fi's nightstand into Pe's big mug of coffee. They're all sitting around the table and the breakfast ceremony can begin; at first the office workers do nothing but watch Pe's mug. But Pe and Fi are focused on that first meal of the day, and neither of them notices their looks. But to judge from the delicacies they start heaping onto their plates, the office workers themselves seem to forget the matter. When they finish, Gill clears the table and Cho washes the dishes. Gong and Gruner declare they're going to straighten up the rooms and make the beds, and under Fi's permissive smile they withdraw.

They'd agreed that all four would meet in Gruner's room once they'd pulled off the first part of the plan. Once there, the office workers—or rather, Gill and Cho, not Gong and Gruner—find themselves feeling nostalgic. Gill believes that, after all, Fi has been like his mother, and Cho admits that he has learned a lot about country living under the tutelage of a man like Pe. The hours of teamwork and the family breakfasts won't be easily forgotten. Gong and Gruner keep moving as these ruminations take place: they pack some bags with a few little souvenirs, some small stones and other things Gill and Cho have collected, plus some apples to eat on the train.

Then Gong's watch alarm goes off: it's time. The train will be here soon, because this is the exact moment when, every day, Pe gets up from the sofa where he does his morning reading and walks to the field to stand beside the tracks and signal. Gruner gets to his feet, and so does Gong, and now everything is in their hands. Gill and Cho will wait on the station bench. In the living room they find Pe asleep on his sofa. They try strong, loud words: "Chomp!" "Attention!" "Scrutinize!" But Pe, sunk into the deep sleep the sedatives induced, doesn't wake up. Gill kisses him on the forehead and Cho imitates him; there are farewell tears in his eyes. Gong makes sure that Fi is in the backyard watering her plants like every morning, and there she is. "Perfect," they say to one another, and finally they all leave the house. Gill and Cho go toward the station, Gong and Gruner toward the field, walking along the tracks toward the train. They spot smoke on the horizon from a train they still can't see, but that can already be heard.

After several steps, Gong stops. Gruner is supposed to go on alone—it takes only one man for the non-signal. After Gong slaps him on the back a few times, Gruner keeps walking. It's going to be hard to see the train approach and want it to stop, and count only on the non-signal. To stand by the tracks and do nothing, to just pray, as Gill said, because maybe that's the signal for God to stop the train.

The train comes closer, moving along one of the two tracks that cross the countryside from one horizon to the other. And soon it's at the station. Gruner focuses. He stays as still as possible, and when the train passes him, it's hard for him to tell if that's the sound of a train speeding up or of one that's going to stop. Then he moves his eyes down toward the wheels turning along the tracks, and he notices that the iron arms that push it along are starting to slow their movement. He doesn't see Gong, doesn't know where he is, but he hears his shouts of joy. The train moves past him and, finally, comes to a complete stop in the station. Gruner watches triumphantly as the station begins to fill up with passengers, but finally he realizes that, underneath the clamor of people, Gong's cries are directed at him: he is very far from the station, and the train's whistle is already announcing its departure. Gruner starts to run.

At the station, in order to board the train, Gill and Cho have to push through dozens and dozens of passengers who are still disembarking. People and luggage are everywhere. The same words are repeated like an echo along the length of the whole train platform:

"I thought we'd never get off."

"Years, years, I've been on this train, but today, at last . . ."

"I don't even remember the town anymore, and now, suddenly, we're here . . ."

People shout and cheer, there's almost no more room in the station. Then there's another whistle, and the sound of the train as it starts to move off. Gruner is almost there. He sees Gong waiting at the end of the platform to help him up, and he jumps the steps. A group of men who have unpacked their instruments play a happy tune to celebrate the occasion. Gong and Gruner move among children, men, and women, and before they can reach the first door, the train is already moving alongside them. That's when Gruner sees, among jubilant ex-passengers, the thin gray figure of the dog.

"Gruner!" yells Gong, who has now reached the first door.

"I'm not going without the dog," declares Gruner, and as if those words give him the strength he needs, he goes back to the animal and picks him up. The dog lets him do it, and his terrified face goes with Gruner as he dodges the euphoric bodies. They reach the train's last car and pull even with it. Gruner senses that from one of the windows Gill and Cho are watching him in anguish, and he knows he can't fail them. He grabs hold of the back stairs of the train and the thrust of the machine plucks him from the platform, as though from a memory in which their feet had recently been planted, but that now grows smaller and disappears in the countryside.

The back door of the car opens and Gong helps Gruner up. Inside, Gill and Cho take the dog and congratulate Gruner. The four—now five—of them are there, and they're saved. But, and there is always a *but*, in the door there is a window, and from that window they can still make out their station. A station full of happy people, overflowing with office supplies and probably also with change. It's a stain that for them has been a place of bitterness and fear and that nevertheless now, they imagine, is something like the happy civilization of the capital. A final feeling, shared by all, is of fear: the sense that, when they reach their destination, there will be nothing left.

OLINGIRIS

There was space for six. One didn't get in, and she was left pacing the waiting room. It took her a while to digest the fact she
would have to live with the urge until the next day, or the next,
or whenever they finally called her in again. It wasn't the first
time this had happened to her. The ones who did make it in went
up the white steps to the second floor. None of them knew one
another, not really. Maybe their paths had crossed, perhaps in
that very place, but no more than that. They filed silently into

the changing rooms. They hung up their purses, shed their coats. They took turns washing their hands and alternated in front of the mirrors, pulling back their hair in headbands or tying it into ponytails. All politely and in silence, thanking one another with gestures or smiles. They've been thinking about this all week. While they worked, while they cared for their children, while they ate, and now here they are. Almost inside the room, now almost about to start.

One of the institute's assistants opens the door to the room and ushers them in. Inside, everything is white. The walls, the shelves, the towels rolled up like tubes, stacked. The cot in the center. The six chairs around it. There is also a gently spinning ceiling fan, six silver tweezers lined up on a towel spread over a wooden stool, and a woman lying on the cot. The six women settle into the chairs, three on each side around the woman's legs. They wait, looking at the body impatiently, unsure what to do with their hands, as if they were at a table where the food had finally been served but they weren't allowed to start eating yet. The assistant circles them, helps them draw their chairs closer. Then she distributes the towels and hands out the six tweezers that were on the stool. The woman on the cot remains motionless, facedown. She is naked. A white towel covers her from the waist to mid-thigh. Her head is hidden in her crossed arms, because it's better if they don't see her face. Her hair is blond, her body thin. The assistant turns on the fluorescent light over the cot, some two yards up, and it illuminates the room and the woman even more. When the tube flickers slightly before turning on completely, the woman on the cot moves her arms a bit, as though settling in, and two of the women watch her reproachfully.

When the assistant gives the signal to begin, the women fold the hand towels into quarters and place the small squares of cloth in front of them, on the cot. Then they scoot their chairs even closer, or they rest their elbows on the cot, or smooth their hair back one last time. And they get to work. They hold the tweezers poised over the woman's body, quickly choose a hair, and lower them, open, decisive. They close, pinch, yank. The dark bulb comes out clean and perfect. They study it a second before leaving it on the towel, then go for the next one. Six seagulls' beaks pulling fish from the sea. The hair in the tweezers fills them with pleasure. Some of them do the work to perfection. The whole hair hangs from the tweezers, orphaned and useless. Others struggle a bit with the task and have to try more than once. But nothing deprives them of their pleasure.

The assistant circles the table. She makes sure the women are all comfortable, that none of them lack for anything. Every once in a while, a pull, a pinch, provokes a slight tremor in the legs. Then the assistant stops short and turns her gaze to the woman on the cot. She rues the institute's regulations that have the subjects lie facedown, because with the woman's head hidden she can't reprimand her with a look. But she has her notepad, which she takes from the pocket of her smock, and she efficiently records the infractions. The woman on the cot hears the squeak of the rubber sandals stopping short. She knows what that means. Sooner or later enough marks accumulate and her pay is docked. The legs are gradually covered with little pink dots. Now they almost don't tremble, because the pulling puts the irritated skin to sleep; now there is only a gentle burn.

When the woman on the cot was ten years old, she lived with her mother near the river. It was an area that sometimes flooded and forced them to go to her aunt's house, a few yards up the hill and built on wooden stilts. Once, when the woman on the cot was doing her homework in her aunt's dining room, she looked out the window and saw a fisherman prowling around the other house, her mother's house. He had arrived in a boat that he'd tied to some trees. Some high boots protected him from the water, which almost reached his knees. She saw him disappear around one side of the house and then appear on the other. He looked in through the windows. But at no point did he knock on the door or on the glass. He waited until the door of the house opened and her mother, first looking around to be sure no one saw him, let him in. The woman on the cot could watch them if they stayed close to the window. Her mother offered him hot tea, and they sat at the table. Then they left the kitchen. When the woman on the cot returned home from the other house, the fisherman was voraciously eating his supper while he entertained her mother with anecdotes about his work and the river. The fisherman offered to take the woman on the cot fishing the next day. Since it was flood season and there was no school, the mother thought it was a good idea. The fisherman took her as far as the river's mouth, where it emptied into the lake. At that point the boat almost didn't move, it glided gently over the mirror of water and her fear slowly left her. It was only just beginning to dawn.

The fisherman assembled his rod, placed the bait on the line, and started to work. At that point she realized she was cold and hungry, but when she asked if her mother had made something for their breakfast, the fisherman made a *tsk-tsk* sound and motioned her to be quiet. She asked if he had an extra coat in the boat. The fisherman *tsk*ed again.

"Are you my father?" she asked finally.

The fisherman sat looking at her, and she got it into her head to smile. But he said:

"No."

And they said nothing more.

The mother of the woman on the cot always had wanted her daughter to study and move to the city. She demanded her daughter get good grades, and she made sure to repeat that if she didn't try hard now, she would pay for it later, and it would be costly. The woman on the cot studied. She did everything her mother told her. The school was two miles from the house and she traveled there by bike. When it flooded, the school called to assign her homework. In high school she learned typing, English, basic computing. On her way home one afternoon, the chain on her bicycle broke. The woman on the cot fell into the mud and the notebooks she was carrying in the basket were ruined. A boy who was driving a truck down the road saw her fall, caught up with her, and got out to help. He was very nice. He gathered up her notebooks and wiped them off on his coat sleeves, and he offered to take her home. They loaded the bike into the truck bed. They talked a little during the drive. She told him what she was studying, and that she was preparing to move to the city. He seemed interested in everything she said. He had a very fine gold chain hanging around his neck with a small cross on it. It seemed beautiful to her. She didn't believe in God, and her mother didn't either, but something made her think her mother would like him. When they arrived she invited him to come to dinner later with them. He seemed delighted, but said:

"It's just that I have to go to work in a while. I'm a fisherman." He smiled. "Can I come tomorrow?"

"No," she said. "I don't think tomorrow is a good idea. I'm sorry."

When the woman on the cot went to the city, she was twenty years old. She was pleased to see that the houses weren't raised on wooden stilts, so floods and fishermen were ruled out. The city also seemed warm to her, and it made her a little dizzy those first days. On Sundays she called her mother and told her some things about her week. Sometimes she lied. She didn't do it out of malice, but rather to distract herself. She told her mother that she'd gone out with new friends. Or that she'd gone to the movies. Or that she'd eaten some delicious food in a neighborhood restaurant. The mother seemed to love these stories. And sometimes she couldn't wait to hang up, so she could repeat them over the phone to the aunt as well.

The woman on the cot had some savings and had signed up at a community college. But the expenses of food, rent, and school were very high, and soon she had to interrupt her studies and look for a job. One afternoon she was out buying bread, and the woman at the shop, to whom she sometimes told her problems, said that she had just the job for her. She said it would pay good money and leave her plenty of time to study. The woman on the cot wasn't stupid. She knew the job could involve something unpleasant that no one else would want to do, or that it could be dangerous. She said she couldn't make any promises, but she was interested in finding out what it was.

The shop owner drove her to a nearby avenue and stopped in front of a two-story building with a sign that said INSTITUTE. Inside, there was a small throng of women. One of them, wearing a peach-colored uniform that also said "Institute," asked the women to form a straight line, and threatened not to reserve a turn for them if they were disorderly. The women quickly got organized. Another woman in a uniform recognized the shop owner and came right over to them. She led them into another room and asked the woman on the cot to roll up her pants so she could see the hair on her legs. At first the woman on the cot thought she hadn't understood the request. But it was repeated. Then she thought it was ridiculous, and that this was surely not a job for her. But neither did she see the danger in showing her leg hair to the uniformed woman, so she rolled up her pant leg and showed her. The woman in uniform put on her glasses and studied the hairs, taking a small flashlight from her pocket and shining it on them. She assessed the ankle, where the hairs were not very thick, and also the calf. Only when she seemed convinced that the woman on the cot would do did she explain the job, giving a general description and the salary. The woman on the cot didn't know what to say. The job was very simple and the pay was acceptable. Her mother had talked to her so much about the traps that were everywhere in the city that she tried for some seconds to figure out where the danger or the deception could be. But it still seemed like a fine offer. And she accepted.

When there are no more hairs left, the legs look red and raw. The woman on the cot doesn't move. The six women around the legs look tired but satisfied. They lean back in their chairs, sigh, rest their hands in their laps. The assistant gathers up the hand towels where the women collected the hairs. Before picking them up, she folds them in half twice so that none of the hairs are lost, and she deposits them carefully into a bag that she closes with a double knot once it's full. Only then does she help the women stand up, pulling back their chairs, sometimes adjusting their shirt collars or any shoulder pads that may have shifted out of place. Then she picks up the bag, delicately, taking care not to tip it, opens the door, and goes with the women to the changing room. When they are all inside, the assistant goes back into the hall and closes the door behind her. Sometimes the women comment on the shift, laugh, or ask questions about previous sessions, and the assistant listens to them chat as she goes down the white stairs. She knows she must store the bag safely before returning to the woman on the cot.

The assistant was born in the country, in a family that made its living from crops and vineyards. They had an estate with a large main house surrounded by gardens, and a small fortune. The assistant liked fish, and her father, who was almost never home, used to send her enormous books with color illustrations of all the fish in the world. She learned their names and drew them in her notebook. Of all the fish, her favorite was one called the Olingiris. Its body was short and thin, it had a long, tube-shaped mouth, and it was turquoise and yellow. The books said it was a delicate fish, because it ate only coral polyps, and those weren't found just anywhere. She asked for one, but it was explained to her that they couldn't have a pet fish in the countryside. The assistant showed her mother a book that explained how to install and maintain a fish tank, but the mother told her that even if they got the tank and the right food, the fish would die of sadness. The assistant thought perhaps her father wouldn't have the same opinion, that maybe she could show him the pictures and he would understand. But when he finally came home, she couldn't find the book anywhere.

The assistant had many brothers, but they were older and worked with her father, so she spent most of the day alone. When she turned seven, she started attending a rural school. One of the men who worked for her father came to pick her up at seven-thirty, dropped her off at school at eight, and came back for her at twelve. It wasn't easy for the assistant to adapt to that new rhythm. At first she didn't do well. Then her mother hired a private tutor, and the assistant started to study in the mornings at school and at home in the afternoons. The private tutor knew of the assistant's interest in fish, and she built her exercises around that subject. Sometimes she read poetry, and once when they were studying punctuation she proposed that the assistant write some verses. The assistant gave it a try, and the tutor seemed delighted with the result. As homework, she assigned the assistant to write a poem with the names of her favorite fish. The assistant cleared off her desk and set out just a few blank sheets of paper, a pencil, and an eraser. She wrote a poem about fish, but invented fish. She wrote about what she felt sometimes in the morning, when she was just waking up and sometimes didn't fully know who she was or where. About the things that made her happy, about the things that didn't, and about her father.

One afternoon the tutor told the assistant that she had a surprise for her, and she took a very large package from her bag, the size of a folder or bigger, and gift-wrapped. Before letting her open it, she made the assistant promise that it would be a secret, and that she would never tell anyone about the gift. The assistant agreed. She tore off the paper, and when she saw what it was, she thought her whole life wouldn't be long enough to repay the tutor for this gift. It was the book about fish and fish tanks. Not the same one, but one just like it, new, identical.

By the time she turned twelve the assistant's level had improved a lot, and her mother decided the private tutor was no longer necessary. For a while, the assistant drew her among the fish. She made some drawings of the tutor kissing the Olingiris, and another of the tutor pregnant with an Olingiris's baby. She wrote some poems for her mother to send to the tutor, and her mother promised to mail them, but there was never a reply.

When the assistant finished high school, she started to manage her father's finances and to oversee some things in the fields. She didn't paint or write anymore, but on her desk she had a framed photo of the Olingiris, and sometimes, when she was taking a break, she picked it up to look at it closely, and she wondered what the private tutor was doing, and what it was like to live the way an Olingiris lived.

She didn't get married or have children. She left the country-side when her mother started showing the first symptoms of ill-ness, the same year the drought finished off the vineyards and the crops. It was decided the assistant would travel with her mother to the capital, and they would live in the apartment her father had bought there some years before. The assistant brought the book about fish and fish tanks that the tutor had given her. The apartment wasn't very large, but it was enough for the two of them. It had a window that looked out onto a street and let in a bit of light. They bought a table and two beds made of pine, and the assistant tore some pages from the book and stuck them to the wall like framed pictures. The assistant learned to cook, to make the beds and wash the clothes. She found work in a dry cleaner's. Once the clothes were clean, they had to be put into the steamer, making sure there were no wrinkles. Lower the lid, wait a few seconds, and repeat on the rest of the garment. She also had to fold and perfume it. Sometimes there were difficult stains, and she had to bring them to the sinks in the back and use a special product. When that happened, the assistant chose the first sink, and while she waited the ten seconds the product needed to work, she looked into her own eyes in the mirror.

When the assistant's mother died, she quit her job, and as she was reorganizing the apartment, she found the book about fish among her mother's clothes. It was the original one, the one that had been lost. She cleared off the pine table and opened the two books to the first page. She reread them side by side, several times. She thought that perhaps she could find a difference, because at first glance they looked the same, but she remembered the first one differently. It was hard to explain; she was just sure that there had to be a difference, but she couldn't find it. She closed the books and sat looking at them for a while. She wouldn't need them anymore, she concluded, and she stored them away together under the bed.

She waited several days at home, with no mother and no job, not really knowing what to do. When the food and money ran out, she left the apartment to walk around the neighborhood, and she came across a "Help Wanted" sign on a building that said INSTITUTE. The work was simple, and paid well. She was hired immediately. The money from the first months left her enough to paint the apartment and buy some furniture. She threw away the pages hanging on the walls. She went out in the morning in her uniform and walked to the institute. She unlocked the doors, filled out forms, went with the women to the changing room, opened the hall, set out the materials, monitored the woman on the cot, collected the hairs, tied the bag, delivered the bag, sent the women on their way, paid the woman on the cot, turned out the lights, locked the door. At home she organized the groceries, made dinner, ate in front of the TV, washed the dishes, showered, brushed her teeth, made the bed, and lay down to sleep. Sometimes the forms ran out and she had to go to the stationery store for more.

Or the women on the cot moved and she had to discount points from their salaries. Or she couldn't find what she wanted to eat for dinner, and she went to bed earlier than usual.

———

The assistant went to reception and saw through the window that it was nighttime. She put the bag away in a cabinet under the counter alongside three other identical bags, and she locked the cabinet. When she opened it the next day they would be gone. Someone would come for them after she left. In the city, everything unseemly moved at night.

The women came downstairs in their street clothes and said goodbye before going outside. That left only the woman on the cot, who must be dressed now and waiting for her upstairs. She went up and opened the hall again, and was surprised to see that the woman on the cot was still naked. She was sitting on the cot, hugging her knees with her forehead on her arms. Her back shuddered. She was crying. It was the first time this had ever happened, and the assistant didn't quite know what to do. She thought about leaving the room and coming back a few minutes later, but instead she took out her notebook, went over the accounts aloud, and handed the woman on the cot the ticket with her money. Then the woman on the cot looked at her, for the first time. And the assistant felt an impulse, her stomach contracted a little, mechanically, her lungs took in air, her lips opened, her tongue hung in the air, waiting, as if she were going to ask the woman on the cot a question. A question like what? That was what closed her mouth. Was she all right? All right in what respect? In no way was she going to ask the question, though the distance between their bodies was appropriate and they were alone in the building; it was just something slow-moving in her head. But it was the woman on the cot who steadied her breathing and said:

"Are you all right?"

The assistant waited. She wanted to see what happened, to understand what was happening, what it was exactly that she was being asked. She felt something intense in her throat, a sharp pain that brought up the image of the books on the pine table, the pages of the two Olingirises, one next to the other, and as if it were a second chance, she looked desperately for a difference, in the eyes, in the scales, in the fins, the colors.

MY BROTHER WALTER

My brother Walter is depressed. My wife and I visit him every night after work. We buy something to eat—he's partial to chicken and french fries —and ring his bell around nine. He comes to the door right away and asks, "Who is it . . . ?" My wife says, "It's us!" and he says, "Oh . . ." and lets us in.

He has a dozen people a day call him to see how he is. He always picks up the phone with effort, as if it weighs a ton, and says:

"Yes?"

And the people talk as though my brother fed off stupidity. If I ask him who it is or what they want, he's incapable of answering. He's not interested in the slightest. He is so depressed that it doesn't even bother him that we're there, because it's the same as if he were alone.

Some Saturdays, my mother and Aunt Claris take him to events at the assembly hall, and Walter sits there amid the forty-something birthday girls, the bachelors, and the newlyweds. Aunt Claris, who always looks for the most arcane side of the simplest things, says that the more depressed Walter is, the happier people around him feel. Now, that's really dumb. What is true, though, is that for a few months now things in our family have been improving.

For instance, my sister finally married Galdós. At the reception, among a group of people at my brother's table drinking champagne and crying with laughter, my mother met Mr. Kito, and now she lives with him. Mr. Kito has cancer, but the man has a lot of energy. He's always enthusiastic, and he's very attentive with my mother. He owns a large cereal company, and he's also a childhood friend of Aunt Claris's. Galdós and my sister bought a farm far from the city, and we've all gotten into the habit of spending weekends there. My wife and I go pick up Walter first thing on Saturday, and by noon everyone is at the farm, waiting by the grill with a glass of wine and that immense happiness that comes with sunny days in fresh air.

We've missed only one weekend so far, because Walter had the flu and refused to get into the car. I felt like I should let the others know he wasn't going, and then everyone started calling everyone else, wondering if it was worth meeting up without him. By the time Galdós was serving up the barbecue, we had all backed out of the event.

Now Aunt Claris is dating the foreman at the farm and we're all couples in the family, except for Walter, of course. There's a chair near the grill that he claimed the first day we brought him, and he doesn't get up from it. Maybe he likes it because it's always in the shade. We try to stay around him, to cheer him up or keep him company. We take pains to talk about more or less superficial subjects, and always optimistically. My sister and my wife, who get along marvelously, comment on the week's news. And there is always occasion to raise a glass to Kito for the encouraging results of his cancer treatment, or Galdós for the profit his farm is making, or my mother because, quite simply, we adore her.

But time passes, and Walter's still depressed. He wears a baleful expression, sadder and sadder all the time. Galdós brings a well-known rural doctor to the farm, and right away he takes an interest in Walter's case. He asks for a chair and sits down facing Walter. He wants privacy, so we leave them alone for a while. We wait on the covered porch of the house. We chat surreptitiously, appetizers in hand, until the doctor comes back from the shade. He looks confident. I tell him he looks young, stupendously healthy, and he tells me the same. He says that Walter needs time, but that he has faith things will work out. So, we all like the doctor. We consult one another on the phone during the week and everyone agrees he seems like a great guy, and we invite him to the farm more often to refine Walter's treatment. He doesn't charge us anything. His wife comes along, too, and she chats with my wife and my sister, and they all agree to meet downtown to go to the movies or the theater together. Then it happens that the rural doctor, Kito, and Galdós get to chatting pleasantly around Walter, smoking and making silly comments to cheer him up a little, and they end up having a long conversation about business. The three of them start a new line of cereals at Kito's company but through Galdós's farm, with a healthier recipe the doctor develops with great success, over the following weeks. I join the project as well and I have to be at the farm almost every day, so when my wife gets pregnant, we move out to the farm, too. We bring Walter, who voices practically no opinion about the changes. We're relieved to have him here with us, relieved to see him sitting in his chair, to know he's close by.

The new cereals sell very well, and the farm fills up with workers and wholesale buyers. The people are friendly. They seem to be very pleased with how we do things and the prices we charge. We're spurred by an optimistic energy that continues to have its most glorious moments on the weekends, when the meat starts to brown on the grill at Galdós's ever more crowded barbecue, as we all eagerly await the food with our wineglasses in hand. We're doing things well. And by now there are so many of us that Walter is almost never alone for a second. We're comforted to know that there's always someone vying for the seat the doctor left beside him in the shade, always someone eager to cheer him up, eager to tell him good news, to make him see how happy a person can come to be if they really put their mind to it.

The business grows. Kito's cancer is finally cured, and my son turns two years old. When I put him in Walter's arms, my son smiles and claps and says, "I'm happy, I'm so happy." Aunt Claris travels with the foreman. A tour of the European Mediterranean keeps them entertained for two months. When they come back they feel even closer to my sister and to Galdós, who are coming back from the Mexican coast, and the four of them spend afternoons exchanging photos. Some nights they go to the casino, and every time they go they win a lot of money. That's how we do things. With the money and some advice from the foreman, they form a company and buy out the cereal lines of the competition. For New Year's, the company invites almost the entire town surrounding the farm—because by now almost everybody works here—and the wholesale purchasers, friends, and neighbors. The barbecue happens at night. No one needs to bring anything; we have everything to give. A live band plays that kind of jazz from the thirties that makes you dance even sitting down. The kids play with garlands, winding them around the chairs and tables, laughing at everything.

For a while now I've been taking my brother aside every so

often, when I can find a calm moment, to ask him what's wrong. He stays quiet as always, but he automatically stops looking me in the eyes. I think it'll be hard to ask him right now, because it's midnight on the dot and we're setting off fireworks as we toast, the kind that light up the whole sky, and people shout and clap and ask for more. I see Walter sitting in his chair, Walter's back, and I see my son run past him, dragging his garland. But he lets go and it falls. He notices right away, and he turns around to look for it. Then something new happens: Walter leans over and picks it up. His motion strikes me as uncanny, and I can't move or say anything. Walter looks at the garland, seeming to study it with too much attention, and for a moment everything seems confused to me. Gray. Paralyzed. It's only a moment, because then my son takes the garland from Walter and goes running back to his mother. Although I recognize the relief, my legs are shaking. I almost feel like we could die, all of us, for some reason, and I can't stop thinking about what's wrong with Walter, what it is that could be so terrible.

THE MERMAN

I'm sitting at the bar in the port, waiting for Daniel, when I see the merman look at me from the pier. He's sitting on the first concrete column, where the water is deeper and the beach hasn't begun, some fifty yards out. It takes me a minute to realize what I'm seeing, what he is exactly: such a man from the waist up, such a sea creature from the waist down. He looks to one side, then calmly to the other, and finally his eyes turn back to me.

My first impulse is to stand up. But I know that the Italian, the owner of the place, is a friend of Daniel's, and he's watching me from the bar. So instead I shift the things on the table around, looking for the bill for my coffee, as if from one moment to the next I'd decided to leave. The Italian comes over to see if everything is okay, he insists I stay, that Daniel must be almost here and I have to wait. I tell him to take it easy, I'll be right back. I leave five pesos on the table, pick up my purse, and leave. I don't have a plan for the merman, I just leave the bar and walk in his direction. Contrary to the idea people have of mermaids, beautiful and tanned, not only is this one of the opposite sex, he's also quite pale. But he's solid, muscular. When he sees me, he crosses his arms—his hands under his armpits, thumbs up—and smiles. It strikes me as too much swagger for a merman, and I regret that I'm walking toward him so confidently, with such a desire to talk to him, and I feel stupid. He waits for me to get closer—it's too late to go back—and he says:

"Hi."

I stop.

"What's a babe like you doing alone on this dock?"

"I thought maybe . . ." I don't know what to say. I let my purse fall from my shoulder and hold it with both hands so it hangs in front of my knees. "I thought maybe you needed something, since you . . ."

"Come join me, beautiful," he says, and he reaches out a hand to invite me up.

I look at his legs, or more like his shining tail that hangs down over the concrete. I pass him my purse; he takes it, places it next to him. I put one foot against the pier and take the hand he offers me again. His skin is cold, like a fish from the freezer. But the sun is high and strong, and the sky an intense blue, and the air smells clean, and when I settle in next to him I feel the coolness of his body fill me with a vital happiness. I'm embarrassed, and I let go of him. I don't know what to do with my hands. I smile. He smooths his hair—he has a pompadour, very American—and asks if I have a cigarette. I tell him I don't smoke. His skin is silky, not a single hair on his whole body, and it's covered in little halos of white dust, barely visible, maybe left by the sea salt. He sees me looking at him and he brushes a little from his arms. He has very defined ab muscles. I've never seen a belly like his.

"You can touch me," he says, caressing his abs. "You don't see *these* downtown, now do you?"

I put out my hand; he catches it and presses it against his abs, also cold. He holds me like that a few seconds, then says:

"Tell me about yourself." And he lets me go, gently. "How is everything?"

"Mom is sick, the doctors don't think she'll hold on much longer."

We look out at the ocean together.

"How terrible . . ." he says.

"But that's not the problem," I say. "It's Daniel I'm worried about. Daniel's in bad shape and that doesn't help."

"He can't accept what's happening with your mother?"

I nod.

"Just the two siblings?"

"Yes."

"At least you can divide things between you. I'm an only child and my mother is very demanding."

"There are two of us, but he does everything. I need to stay rested. I can't allow myself strong emotions. I have a problem here, in my heart; I think it's my heart. So I keep my distance. For my health . . ."

"And where is Daniel now?"

"He's always late. He spends all day running around. He has a big problem with time management."

"What sign is he? Pisces?"

"Taurus."

"Oh! Tough sign."

"I have some mints," I say. "Want one?"

He says yes and hands me my purse.

"He spends all day thinking about where he's going to get money to pay for this thing and where for that one. All the time wanting to know what I'm doing, where I'm going to be, who I'm with . . ."

"Does he live with your mother?"

"No. Mom is like me, we're independent women and we need our space. He thinks it's dangerous for me to live alone. He says it just like that: 'I think it's dangerous for a girl *like you* to live alone.' He wants to pay a woman to follow me around all day. Of course, I never agreed to that."

I hand him a mint and take one for myself.

"You live around here?"

"He rents a house for me a few blocks away: he thinks this neighborhood is much safer. And he makes friends around here, talks to the neighbors, the Italian. He wants to know everything, control everything—he's really unbearable."

"My father was like that."

"Yeah, but he's not Dad. Dad is dead. Why do I have to deal with a father-brother, when Dad's dead?"

"Well, maybe he's just trying to look out for you."

I laugh sarcastically. Really, the comment almost ruins my mood, and I think he realizes it.

"No, no. It's not about looking out for me, it's more complicated than you think."

He sits looking at me. His eyes are very light, sky blue.

"Tell me."

"Ah, no. Believe me, it's not worth it: it's a beautiful day."

"Please."

He presses his hands together, begs me with a funny face, like an angel about to cry. Sometimes, when he talks to me, the fin at the tip of his silvered tail waves a little and brushes against my ankles. The scales are rough, but they don't hurt, it's a pleasant feeling. I don't say anything, and the fin gets closer.

"Tell me . . ."

"It's just that Mom . . . She's not just sick: the truth is, the poor woman is totally crazy . . ."

I sigh and look up at the sky. The light-blue, absolute sky. Then we look at each other. For the first time I look at his lips. Are they cold, too? He takes my hands, kisses them, and says:

"Do you think we could go out? You and me, one of these days . . . We could go to dinner, or the movies. I love movies."

I kiss him, and I feel the cold of his mouth awaken every cell in my body, like a cool drink in the middle of summer. It's not just a sensation, it's a revelatory experience, because I feel like nothing can ever be the same again. But I can't tell him I love him: not yet, more time has to pass, we have to take things step-by-step. First he comes to the movies, then I go to the bottom of the sea. But I already made a decision, irrevocable, and now nothing will separate me from him. Me, who my whole life believed one lives for a single love—I found mine on the pier, beside the sea. And now he takes me frankly by the hand, and he looks at me with his transparent eyes, and he tells me:

"Stop suffering, baby, no one's going to hurt you anymore."

A car horn honks in the distance, from the street. I recognize it right away: it's Daniel's car. I look over my merman's shoulder. Daniel gets out in a hurry and goes straight toward the bar. Apparently he hasn't seen me.

"I'll be right back," I say.

He hugs me, kisses me again. "I'll wait for you," he says. He lets me use his arm as a rope to climb down more easily, and he hands me my purse.

I run to the bar. Daniel is talking to the Italian when he sees me.

"Where were you? We said we'd meet at your house, not at the bar."

It's not true, but I don't say anything. It's not important now.

"I need to talk to you," I say.

"Let's go to the car, we'll talk in the car."

He takes my arm, gently, but with that paternal attitude that irritates me so much, and we leave. The car is a few yards away, but I stop.

"Let go of me."

He lets go but keeps walking to the car, and he opens the door.

"Let's go, it's late. The doctor's going to kill us."

"I'm not going anywhere, Daniel."

Daniel stops.

"I'm going to stay here," I say, "with the merman."

He stands looking at me for a second. I turn back toward the ocean. He, beautiful and silver on the pier, raises an arm and waves at us. And even so, Daniel gets into the car and opens the door on my side. Then I don't know what to do, and when I don't know what to do, the world seems like a terrible place for someone like me, and I feel very sad. That's why I think, *He's just a merman, he's just a merman,* as I get into the car and try to calm down. He could be there tomorrow, waiting for me.

RAGE OF PESTILENCE

Gismondi found it odd that the children and the dogs didn't run out to greet him when he arrived. Disturbed, he looked out over the plain at the car, now tiny, that wouldn't be back for him until the next day.

He had been visiting border places for years, poor communities that he added to the census and remunerated with food. But for the first time, facing that little town sunken in the valley, Gismondi perceived an absolute stillness. He saw only a few houses. Three or four motionless figures, and a few dogs stretched out on the ground. He advanced under the noonday sun. He was carrying two big bags on his shoulders, and as the bags slid down, they dug into his arms and forced him to stop. A dog lifted its head to watch him, but didn't get up from the ground. The buildings, a strange mix of mud, stone, and tin, were arranged in no particular order, leaving an empty street in the middle of the town. The place seemed uninhabited, but he could sense the townspeople behind the windows and doors. They didn't move; they weren't watching him; they were just there, and Gismondi saw, next to a door, a man sitting down; the back of a little boy leaning against a post; a dog's tail poking out from the doorway of a house.

Dizzy from the heat, he dropped the bags and wiped the sweat from his forehead with one hand. He contemplated the buildings. There was no one to talk to, so he chose a house without a door and asked permission to enter before peering in. Inside, an old man was looking at the sky through a hole in the tin roof.

"Excuse me," said Gismondi.

At the other end of the room, two women were facing each other at a table and, behind them, on an old cot, two children and a dog were dozing, their heads and limbs resting on one another.

"Excuse me . . ." he repeated.

The man didn't move. When Gismondi got used to the

darkness, he found that one of the women, the younger one, was looking at him.

"Hello there," he said, recovering his spirits. "I work for the government and . . . Whom should I be talking to?" Gismondi leaned slightly forward.

The woman didn't answer, and her expression was indifferent. Gismondi leaned against the empty doorframe, feeling dizzy.

"You must know someone . . . some kind of leader. Do you know whom I should talk to?"

"Talk?" said the woman in a dry, tired voice.

Gismondi didn't answer; he was afraid of finding that she hadn't uttered a word at all and that the noontime heat was affecting him. The woman seemed to lose interest, and she looked away from him.

Gismondi thought he could estimate the population and complete the record on his own, since no agent would ever bother to check the information in a place like this. But in any case, the car wouldn't be back for him until the next day. He went over to the children, thinking he could at least make them talk. The dog, whose snout was resting on one boy's leg, didn't even move. Gismondi greeted them. Only one of the boys, slowly, looked him in the eyes and made a minimal gesture with his lips, almost a smile. His feet hung from the cot barefoot but clean, as if they had never touched the ground. Gismondi knelt down and brushed one of the feet with his hand. He didn't know what led him to do this; maybe he just needed to know that the boy was capable of movement, that he was alive. The boy looked at him fearfully. Gismondi stood up. His eyes as he looked at the boy also held fear. But it wasn't that face he was afraid of, or the silence, or the lethargy. Then he saw the dust, on the shelves and the empty countertops. He went over to the only container in sight, picked it up, and emptied its contents on the table. He stood there absorbed for some seconds. Then he traced a finger through the spilled powder without understanding what he was seeing. He went through the drawers and the shelves. Opened cans, boxes, bottles. There was nothing. Nothing to eat or to drink. No blankets, no tools, no clothes. Just some useless utensils. Vestiges of jars that had once held something. Without looking at the boys, as if he were talking only to himself, he asked them if they were hungry. No one answered.

"Thirsty?" A shiver made his voice tremble.

They listened to him, although they didn't seem to understand. Gismondi left the room, returned to the street, ran to the bags, and carried them back. He stood in front of the boys, agitated. He emptied the goods onto the table. He picked up a bag at random, opened it with his teeth, and poured a handful of sugar into his palm. The boys watched as he knelt down beside them and offered them something from his hand. But neither of them seemed to understand. It was then that Gismondi felt a presence, and perceived, perhaps for the first time in the valley, the breeze of a movement. He stood up and looked to either side.

A bit of sugar spilled to the ground. The younger woman was standing up now and watching him from the threshold. It wasn't the same expression she'd had up to then—she wasn't looking at a scene or the landscape, she was looking at him.

"What do you want?" she said.

It was, like all the others, a somnolent voice, but it was charged with an authority that surprised him. One of the boys had left the bed and was now looking at the hand overflowing with sugar. The woman looked at the packages spread out on the table and she turned toward him furiously. The dog stood up and restlessly circled the table. Men and women began to look in through the doors and windows, heads appearing behind heads, a growing crowd. Other dogs approached. Gismondi looked at the sugar in his hand. This time, finally, everyone focused their attention on him. He barely saw the boy, his little hand, the wet fingers caressing the sugar, the fascinated eyes, a certain movement of the lips that seemed to remember the sweet taste. When the boy brought his fingers to his mouth, everyone froze. Gismondi retracted his hand. He saw in those who were looking at him an expression that at first he couldn't understand. Then he felt the sharp wound, deep in his stomach. He fell to his knees. He had let the sugar spill, and the memory of hunger spread over the valley with the rage of pestilence.

HEADS AGAINST CONCRETE

If you pound a person's head against concrete—even if you're doing it only so they'll come to their senses—you will very likely end up hurting them. This is something my mother explained to me early on, the day I pounded Fredo's head on the asphalt of the school playground.

I wasn't a violent kid, I want to make that clear. I spoke only if it was strictly necessary, and I didn't have friends or enemies to fight with. The only thing I did at recess was wait in the classroom, alone and far from the noise of the playground, until class started again. While I waited, I drew. It passed the time, and distanced me from the world. I drew locked boxes and fish shaped like puzzle pieces that fit together.

Fredo was the captain of the football team, and in our grade, things happened and were done the way he wanted. He did what he wanted with other people. Like that time Cecilia's uncle died and he made her think he'd done it. That's not good, but I don't stick my nose in other people's problems. One day during recess, Fredo came into the classroom, grabbed the drawing I was working on, and ran out. The drawing was of two puzzle-piece fish, each one in a box, and the two boxes inside another box. I got that thing about the boxes inside of more boxes from a painter Mom likes, and all the teachers loved it and said it was "a very poetic device." On the playground, Fredo was tearing the drawing in half, and the halves in half, and so on, while his friends stood around him and laughed. When he couldn't tear the pieces any smaller, he threw them all into the air. The first thing I felt was sadness. That's not a figure of speech—I always think about how I feel in the moment that things are happening to me, and maybe that's what makes me slower or more distracted than everyone else. Next, my body hardened, I closed my fists and felt my temperature rise. I lunged at Fredo, pulled him down to the ground with me, and grabbed him by the hair. And that was when I started to pound his head against the ground. Our teacher shouted, and another teacher from a different class came to separate us, and nothing else happens in this Fredo story. I'm telling it because I guess that was the start of everything, and when Mom wants to know something she always says, "From the beginning, from the beginning, please!"

In high school I had another "episode." I was still drawing, and no one touched my pictures because they knew I believed in things like good and evil, and the latter category, which is what people in general spent their time on, bothered me. The fight with Fredo had earned me some respect from the class, and they didn't mess with me anymore. But that year there was a new boy who thought he was really smart, and he found out that Cecilia had been indisposed for the first time the day before. And at recess he came into the classroom and filled her pencil case with red paint. I saw it all from my desk, where I was quietly drawing. In the next class, when Cecilia went to get a pen, her fingers and clothes got all stained. And the boy started to yell that she was a whore, that Cecilia was a whore like her mother and all the rest, which in a way also included my mother. I didn't have a crush on Cecilia, but I hit that boy's head against the floor until it started to bleed. The teacher had to call in backup to separate us. While they were restraining us so we wouldn't get into it again, I asked him if his brain was draining a little better now. I thought the phrase was inspired, but I was the only one who laughed. They filled my report card with warnings and suspended me from school for two days. Mom was mad at me, too, but I heard her say over the phone that her son "wasn't used to intolerance and all he wanted to do was protect that poor girl."

From then on Cecilia did everything possible to be my friend. It really got on my nerves to always have her so close, staring at me. She wrote me letters about friendship and love and hid them in my stuff. I went on drawing. My mom had signed me up for the drawing and painting workshop at school, which was every Friday. The teacher sent us to buy paper, much bigger than the kind I'd used until then. Also paints and brushes. The teacher showed my work to the class and explained why I was "so inventive," just how I had accomplished it, and what I "wanted to convey with each brushstroke." In the workshop I learned how to do all of the extremities of puzzle pieces in 3-D, to paint blurred backgrounds that, "against the realism of a horizon, give a sense of abstraction," and to use hairspray on the best pieces so they would be preserved and "the colors wouldn't lose their intensity."

Painting was the most important thing to me. There were other things I liked, such as watching TV, doing nothing, and sleeping. But painting was the best. There was a painting competition in my junior year, and the winning work would be displayed in the lobby. The jury was the drawing teacher, the principal, and her secretary. The three of them "unanimously" chose my work as "the most representative," and they hung my painting in the entrance to the school.

In those days, Cecilia liked to say I was in love with her, and always had been. That the red fish and the blue fish that I'd started to draw between the puzzle pieces was a "romantic abstraction of our relationship." That one fish's puzzle piece fit in with the other's because that's how we were, "made for each other." During a break one day I found that someone had written our names over the fish in the picture; then, on the chalkboard in the classroom, I saw a giant heart pierced by an arrow with our names. It was the same handwriting as on the painting. Everyone had seen it, and they sat looking at one another with rude grins. Cecilia smiled at me, blushing, and again I felt that uncontrollable desire to hit, and even before anything happened I saw the image of her head smashing down, her scalp bashing over and over against the uneven ground, her head splitting open, the blood clumping in her hair. I felt my body lunge at her wildly, and then, for some reason, stop short. It was like an "illumination"—people who know about these things explained it to me much later. And the "illumination" helped me avoid the images I had just seen, and I had the first impulse that led to everything that came after: I ran to the drawing and painting workshop on the second floor—some of the kids, including Cecilia, followed me—and I took paints and paper from the cabinets and sat down to draw. I drew it all. An extreme close-up of the fear in one of Cecilia's terrified eyes, a slice of her sweaty forehead covered with zits and blackheads. The rough ground below her, the tips of my strong fingers just barely in the picture, tangled in her hair, and then red, pure red, staining everything.

If I'm asked what I learned in school, I can reply only that I learned to paint. Everything else went away just as it came, and there's nothing left. Nor did I study anything else after high school. I paint pictures of heads hitting the ground, and people pay me fortunes for them. I live in a loft in downtown Buenos Aires. My bedroom and bathroom are upstairs, the kitchen is downstairs, and all the rest is my studio, or "atelier," as Aníbal likes to call it. Some people ask me for portraits of their own heads. They like gigantic square canvases, and I make them up to six feet by six feet. They pay me whatever I ask. Later I see the paintings hung in their enormous, empty living rooms, and I think that those guys deserve to see themselves good and smashed on the ground by my hand, and they seem very much to agree when they stand in front of the paintings. You'd have to see them to understand what kind of picture I'm talking about. I mean, they're really good pictures.

I don't like to have girlfriends. I dated some girls, but it never worked out. Sooner or later they start to demand more time or ask me to say things I really don't feel. One time I tried saying what I felt, and it was worse. Another time, one of them went completely crazy, and I hadn't said absolutely anything. She decided I didn't love her, that I was never going to love her; she forced me to grab her by the hair and started to hit her own head against the wall. I don't think relationships like that are healthy.

Aníbal, who is my representative and the guy in charge of putting my paintings in galleries and deciding the price of each thing I do, says that the woman thing isn't good for us. He says that masculine energy is superior, because it's not scattered and it is *monothematic*. *Monothematic* means you think about only one thing, but he never says what that thing is. He says that women are fine at first, "when they're really fine," and also at the end, because he saw his father die in his mother's arms and that's a good way to die. But everything in between "is just hell." He says that for now I have to concentrate on what I know how to do, which is saying nothing and painting. He's bald and fat, and no matter what's happening, he's always talking nonstop and panting as if he were out of breath. Aníbal used to be a painter, but he never wants to talk about that. Since I spend all my time in my studio and he persuaded my mom not to bother me, he usually stops by at noon to bring me food and take a look at what I'm working on. He stands in front of the paintings with his thumbs hooked in the front pockets of his jeans, and he always says the same things: "More red, it needs more red." Or: "Bigger, I need to see it from across the street." And almost always, before he leaves: "My man, you're a mega-genius. A me-ga-genius." When I don't feel good because I'm sad or tired, I look in the bathroom mirror, hook my thumbs in my jeans, and tell myself: "You're a mega-genius. A me-ga-ge-nius." Sometimes it works.

And now comes the important part of the story. So, I'd always had a terrible hole between my back right two molars, in my "superior maxilla," and at some point I started getting the food I ate stuck in there. I ended up with some unbearable cavities. Aníbal said I couldn't go to just any dentist, because after women, dentists were the worst. He handed me a business card and said: "He's Korean, but he's good." He got me an appointment for that same afternoon.

John Sohn looked young and I thought maybe he was my age, but it's hard to guess Korean people's ages. He gave me a little anesthesia, drilled my teeth, and filled the holes he'd made with paste. All with a perfect smile and without hurting me at any point. I liked him, so I told him how I painted heads against concrete. John Sohn was silent for a moment, which turned out to be like a moment of "illumination"—which made me think we had something important in common—and he said, "That's just what I've been looking for." He invited me to have dinner in one of those real Korean restaurants. I mean, not a touristy one, but the kind you enter through a little door you wouldn't think led anywhere, and then inside it turns out there's a whole Korean world. Big round tables even if you have only two people, and the menu in Korean, and all the waiters are Korean, and all the customers are Korean. John Sohn chose a traditional dish for me and gave the waiter precise instructions on how to prepare it. John Sohn needed someone to paint a gigantic painting for his waiting room. He said the important thing was the tooth. He wanted to make a deal: I'd paint the picture, and he would fix all my teeth. He explained why he wanted the painting, how it would affect the customers, and the value of advertising in his culture. He talked nonstop, like Aníbal, and I like it when someone else does all the talking. When we finished eating, John Sohn introduced me to some Koreans at the table next to us, and we had coffee with them. Now, I don't speak Korean, so I didn't understand anything. But watching them talk helped me realize that now I had a dentist friend, and I had an important deal with my dentist friend, and that that was very good.

I spent many days working on John's picture, until one morning I woke up on the sofa in the studio, looked at the canvas, and felt a deep gratitude: his friendship had given me my best picture. I called him at his office and John was very happy, I know because when something excites him he talks even faster, and sometimes he talks in Korean. He said he would come over for lunch. It was the first time a friend had come to visit me. I organized the paintings a little, making sure to leave the best ones in view. I picked up my clothes and carried them up to the bedroom, and brought the used plates and glasses to the kitchen. I took food from the fridge and set it out on a tray. When John arrived he looked all around for the picture, but I told him that it "wasn't time yet," and he respected that because Koreans know a lot about respect, or at least that's what he always said. So we sat down to lunch. I asked if he wanted more salt, if he preferred something hot, if I could pour him more soda. But everything was fine with him. I thought how maybe he could come over some night to watch movies or chat about whatever. We could take a photo together to display somewhere, like people do with "family and friends." But I didn't say anything about that yet. John ate and talked. He did it all at once, and it didn't bother me because that's intimacy, it's part of being friends. I don't know how he got on the subject, but he started talking about "Korean kids" and education in his country. Kids start school at six in the morning and they leave at noon the next day; that is, they spend almost a day and a half in school and they have only five hours free, which they use to go home, sleep a little, and return. He said those are the things that distinguish the Koreans from the Argentines, that set them apart from the rest of the world.

I didn't like that, but you can't like everything about a friend, that's what I believe. And I think that all in all, in spite of his comments, we were fine. I smiled. "I want you to see the painting," I told him. We walked to the center of the room. He took a few steps back, calculating the distance, and when I felt the time was right, I pulled off the sheet that covered the picture. John had small, fine hands, like a woman's, and he was always moving them to explain what he was thinking. But his hands stayed still, hanging from his arms like they were dead. I asked what was wrong. He said that the painting was supposed to be about the tooth. That what he wanted was a gigantic painting for his waiting room, a painting of a tooth. He repeated that several times.

We looked at the painting together: the face of a Korean crashing against the black and white tiles of a waiting room very much like John's. My hand isn't there pounding the head, it's falling on its own, and the first thing that hits the gleaming tiles, the thing that receives the whole weight of the fall, is one of the Korean's teeth. It has a vertical crack that, an instant later, will split it right down the middle. I couldn't understand what wasn't working for John—the painting was perfect. And I realized I wasn't willing to change a thing. Then John said that's how it always was at the end of the day, and he started in again on the subject of Korean education. He said we Argentines are slackers. That we don't like to work, and that's why our country is the way it is. That it would never change, because we were how we were, and he left.

Now, that really bothered me. I mean a lot. Because my mother and Aníbal are Argentines, too, and they work a lot, and it bothers me when people talk without knowing what they're talking about. But I told myself that John was my friend. I contained my rage, and I felt very proud of that.

The next day I wrote him an email explaining that I could change whatever he wanted me to change in the painting. I clarified that I didn't agree with him "aesthetically," but I understood that maybe he needed something more "commercial." I waited a couple of days, but John didn't answer. Then I wrote him again. I thought maybe he was offended by something, and I explained that if he was, I needed to know what it was, exactly, because otherwise I couldn't apologize. But John didn't answer that email, either.

Mom called Aníbal and explained to him that this was all happening because I was "very sensitive," and I wasn't prepared for "failure." But that didn't have anything to do with it. After seven days with no word I decided to call John at his office. His secretary answered. "Good morning, sir; no, sir, the doctor isn't in; no, sir, the doctor can't call you back." I asked why, what was wrong, why was John doing this to me, why didn't John want to see me? The secretary was quiet for a few seconds and then said, "The doctor took a few days off, sir," and she hung up on me. That weekend I painted six more pictures of Korean heads splitting open on the concrete, and Aníbal was very excited with the work. He said the "Korean thing" gave "a new feel to the whole series," but I was boiling with fury and also still very sad. And then Aníbal, on the condition I wouldn't abandon my "new wave of inspiration," got me John's home address and telephone number. I called immediately, and a Korean woman answered. I said I wanted to talk to John, and I repeated his name several times. The woman said something I didn't understand, something short and fast. She repeated it. Then a man answered, some other Korean who wasn't John, either, and he also said things that I didn't understand.

So I made a decision, an important one. I wrapped the painting in the sheet, dragged it outside as best I could, waited forever until I caught one of those big taxis with enough room in back for the painting, and I gave the driver John's address. John lived in a Korean world fifty blocks from my neighborhood, full of signs in Korean and of Koreans. The taxi driver asked me if I was sure about the address, and whether I wanted him to wait for me at the door. I told him that wasn't necessary. I paid him and he helped me unload the painting. John's house was old and big. I leaned the painting against the entrance gate, rang the doorbell, waited. There are a lot of things that make me nervous. Not understanding something is one of the worst, and the other worst thing is waiting. But I waited. I think these are the things one does for one's friends. I had talked to Mom a few days earlier and she'd said that my friendship with John suffered from a "cultural gap," too, and that made everything more complicated. I told her that a cultural gap was a thing that John and I could fight. I just needed to talk to him, to find out why he was so angry.

The living room curtain moved. Someone looked out for a second from inside. A woman's voice said "Hello" through the intercom. I said I wanted to see John. "John, no," said the woman, "no." She said other things in Korean, the intercom made some noises, and then everything went silent. I rang again. Waited again. Rang. I heard the bolts in the door, and a Korean man older than John opened it, looked at me, and said: "John, no." He said it angrily, scowling, but without looking me in the eyes, and then shut the door again. I realized I didn't feel well. Something was wrong in me, inside me, something was coming out of its place again, like in the old days. I rang the bell again. I yelled "John!" again, again. A Korean man who was walking on the sidewalk across the street stopped to look. I yelled at the intercom again. I just wanted to talk to John. I yelled his name again. Because John was my friend. Because "gaps" didn't have anything to do with us. Because we were two people, John and I, and that's what having a friend is. I pressed the doorbell again, one long ring, and my finger hurt from pressing so hard. The Korean across the street said something in his language. I don't know what, it was like he wanted to explain something to me. And me, again, *"John, John,"* really loud, like something terrible was happening to me. The Korean came over to me and made a hand gesture to calm me down. I took my hand from the doorbell to change fingers and kept shouting. I heard blinds fall in another house. I felt like I couldn't get enough air. Like I didn't have enough of something.

Then the Korean, he touched my shoulder. His fingers on my shirt. And it was an enormous pain: the cultural gap. My body shook, it shook and I couldn't control it, my body didn't understand things anymore, like in the beginning, like other times. I let go of the painting, which fell facedown onto the sidewalk, and I grabbed the Korean by the hair. A small Korean, skinny and nosy. A shitty Korean who had gotten up at five in the morning for fifteen years to reinforce the cultural gap for eighteen hours a day. I held him by the hair so hard that my nails dug into the palm of my hand. And that was the third time I smashed someone's head against the concrete.

When they ask me if "splitting open the Korean's head on the back of my canvas hides an aesthetic intention," I look up and pretend to think. That's something I learned from watching other artists talk on TV. It's not that I don't understand the question, it's just that I'm really not interested. I have legal problems, a lot of legal problems. Because I don't know how to tell the difference between Koreans and Japanese, or Japanese and Chinese, and every time I see one of any of them, I grab him by the hair and start to slam his head against the concrete. Aníbal got me a good lawyer and he's claiming "insanity," which is when you're crazy, and it's much better in the eyes of the law. People say I'm racist, "a hugely evil" man, but my paintings sell for millions, and I'm starting to think about what my mom always said, which is that the problem with the world is that it's in a great crisis of love. And also that, when it comes down to it, these are not good times for very sensitive people.

THE SIZE OF THINGS

All I knew about Enrique Duvel was that he came from a rich family and that, though he was sometimes spotted out with women, he still lived with his mother. On Sundays, he cruised around the plaza in his convertible, withdrawn or self-absorbed, never looking at or greeting any of his neighbors, and then he would disappear until the following weekend. I'd kept the toy store I'd inherited from my father, and one day I caught Duvel in the street, peering dubiously in through the display window of my shop. I mentioned this to Mirta, my wife, who said that maybe I'd gotten him confused with someone else. But then she saw him herself. Yes, on some afternoons, Enrique Duvel stood outside the toy store for a while, looking in through the window.

The first time he came inside, he seemed irresolute, as though he was ashamed and not at all sure what he was looking for. He stood by the counter and scanned the shelves behind me. I waited for him to speak. He played with his car keys for a bit, and finally he asked for a model-plane kit. I asked him if he wanted me to gift wrap it, but he said no.

He came back several days later. Again, he looked in the window for a while, then came inside and asked for the next model plane in the series. I asked him if he was a collector, but he said no.

On successive visits, he moved on to model cars, ships, and trains. He came almost every week, leaving with something each time. One night, I went outside to close the store's shutters and there he was, alone in front of the window. It must have been around nine at night, and there was no one out on the streets. It took me a minute to recognize him, to understand that this trembling man with a red face and weepy eyes could really be Enrique Duvel. He seemed scared. I didn't see his car, and for a moment I thought he'd been attacked."Duvel? Are you all right?"

He made a confused gesture.

"It's best if I stay here," he said.

"Here at the shop? What about your mother?" I instantly regretted my question, afraid I'd offended him, but he said, "She locked herself in the house with all the keys. She says she doesn't want to see me again."

We looked at each other a moment, not quite knowing what to say.

"I'd best stay here," he repeated.

I knew that Mirta would never agree, but by that point I owed the man almost twenty percent of my monthly earnings, and I couldn't just turn him away.

"But you see, Duvel . . . there's nowhere to sleep here."

"I'll pay for the night," he said. He went through his pockets. "I don't have any money on me . . . But I can work. I'm sure there's something I can do."

Though I knew it wasn't a good idea, I brought him inside. It was dark when we entered. When I turned the display lights on, their reflection gleamed in his eyes. Something told me Duvel wouldn't sleep that night, and I was afraid to leave him alone. I saw a towering stack of boxes full of toys that I hadn't had time to sort through, and I imagined the rich and refined Duvel— the sometime subject of Mirta's girlfriends' gossip—stocking my empty shelves overnight. Giving him the task could bring problems, but at least it would keep him busy.

"Could you deal with those boxes?"

He nodded.

"I'll explain in more detail tomorrow. You just have to

organize the items by type." I went over to the merchandise. "The puzzles with the puzzles, for example. You can see where they go, and just put everything together, there, on the shelves. And if—"

"I understand perfectly," Duvel said, interrupting me.

He walked away from me with his eyes fixed on the floor, making a slight movement with his index finger, as if he wanted to shush someone but felt too humiliated to do it. I was going to tell him how there was just an old armchair in the storage room to sleep on, and to give him some advice about the toilet handle, but I didn't want to bother him anymore. I let him be and left without saying goodbye.

The next day, I got to the store a few minutes early; I was relieved to see that the shop's shutters were up. Only once I was inside did I realize that leaving Duvel there alone had been a tremendous mistake. Nothing was where it belonged. If at that moment a customer had come in and asked for a particular superhero figure, it would have taken me all morning to find it. I remember thinking about Mirta and how I would explain this to her, and also the sudden exhaustion I felt as I calculated the hours it would take me to reorganize everything. Then I realized something else, something so strange that, for a moment, I couldn't take it in: Duvel had reorganized the store chromatically. Modeling clay, decks of cards, crawling baby dolls, pedal cars—they were all mixed together and arranged by color. In the display cases, along the aisles, on the shelves: a subtly shifting rainbow stretched from one end of the store to the other. I still remember that sight as the beginning of disaster. *He has to go*, I thought. *I have to get this man out of the store right now.*

Duvel was looking at me. He was very serious, standing there in front of his great rainbow. I was trying to find the words to say what I wanted when his eyes lit on something behind me. I turned toward the street to see what it was. Outside the window, a woman and her two children were looking into the store. Their hands were pressed to the glass like visors as they talked excitedly about what they saw inside, as if something marvelous were moving through the aisles. It was the start of the school day, and at that hour the block was full of children and parents in a hurry. But they couldn't help stopping in front of the windows, and a crowd grew. By noon, the store was packed: never had business been as good as it was that morning. It was hard to find the things that people asked for, but soon I discovered that I had only to name an item and Duvel would nod and run to get it. He located things with an efficient ease I found disconcerting.

"Call me by my first name," he told me at the end of that long day of work, "if that's all right with you."

The color arrangement drew attention to items that had never stood out before. For example, the green swimming flippers followed the squeaky frogs that occupied the final ranks of turquoise, while the puzzles depicting glaciers—maroon at the earthen base of the photograph—brought the rainbow full circle by joining their snowy peaks with volleyballs and stuffed white lions.

The store didn't close for siesta that day, or any of the following days, and little by little, we started pushing back our closing time. Enrique slept in the store from then on. Mirta agreed that we should set up a space for him in the storage room. At first he had to make do with a mattress on the floor, but soon we found a bed. And once or twice a week, during the night, Enrique reorganized the store. He set up scenes with the giant building blocks; he modified the interior light by constructing intricate walls of toys against the windows; he built castles that stretched across the aisles. It was useless to offer him a salary; he wasn't interested. "It's best if I just stay here," he'd say. "Better than a salary."

He didn't leave the store, or, at least, not that I ever saw. He ate what Mirta sent him: packed meals that started out as slices of bread with cold cuts in the evenings, and later became elaborate lunches and dinners.

Enrique no longer went near the model kits he used to love so much. He put them on the store's highest shelves and there they stayed, always. They were the only things that remained in one spot. Now he preferred puzzles and board games. In the mornings, if I arrived early, I'd find him sitting at the table with a glass of milk, playing with two colors of Chinese checkers or fitting the last pieces of a large fall landscape into place. He'd grown quieter, but he never lost his attentiveness toward the customers. He got into the habit of making his bed in the mornings and cleaning the table and sweeping the floor after he ate. When he was done, he came over to me or to Mirta—who, because of the extra business, had started working behind the counter—and said, "I made my bed," or "I finished sweeping," or even "I finished what I had to do." And it was that manner of his—obsequious, as Mirta called it—that made us start to worry, somehow.

One morning, I found that he had built a small zoo on the table using dolls, farm animals, and Legos. He was drinking his glass of milk while he opened the gate for the horses and made them gallop, one by one, over to a dark sweater that served as a mountain. I greeted him and went to the counter to start working. When he came over to me he seemed embarrassed.

"I already made the bed," he said, "and I finished what—"

"It's okay," I said. "I mean, it doesn't matter if you make the bed or not. It's your room, Enrique."

I thought we were understanding each other, but he looked down at the floor, even more embarrassed, and said, "Sorry, it won't happen again. Thank you."

After a while, Enrique also stopped reorganizing the puzzles and board games. He placed the boxes on the upper shelves alongside the model kits, and retrieved them only if a customer asked for them specifically.

"You have to talk to him," Mirta said. "People are going to think we don't have puzzles anymore. Just because he doesn't use them doesn't mean they're not for sale."

But I didn't say anything. Things were going well with the business, and I didn't want to hurt his feelings.

Over time, he started to reject certain foods. He would eat only meat, mashed potatoes, and pasta with simple sauces. If we gave him anything else, he would push it away, so Mirta started cooking only the things that he liked.

Every once in a while the customers would give him coins, and when he had saved enough he bought from the store a blue plastic cup with a convertible car in relief. He used it at breakfast, and in the morning, when reporting the state of his bed and his room, he began to add, "I also washed my cup."

Mirta told me worriedly that one afternoon she'd been watching Enrique play with a boy who'd come into the store, and he suddenly grabbed a superhero figure and refused to share it. When the boy started to cry, Enrique stomped off and locked himself in the storage room.

"You know how much I care about Enrique," my wife said that night, "but we just can't let him get away with things like that."

Although he still had his genius when it came to reorganizing the merchandise, over time he also stopped playing with the little articulated dolls and the Legos, and he archived them, along with the board games and model kits, on the now overcrowded upper shelves. The range of toys that he still reorganized and kept within the customers' reach was so small and monotonous that it barely attracted the youngest children.

"Why do you put those things up so high, Enrique?" I asked him.

He looked disconsolately at the shelves, as if, in effect, they were too high for him as well. He didn't answer; he was quieter all the time.

Little by little, sales went back down. Enrique's rainbows, displays, and castles lost the splendor of those first days, when almost all the toys participated in his radical remodeling. Now everything happened at knee-level and below. Enrique was almost always hunched over or kneeling in front of a new pile of toys that was ever smaller and more amorphous. The place had started to empty of customers. Soon we didn't need Mirta's help anymore, and Enrique and I were left alone.

I remember the last afternoon I saw Enrique. He hadn't wanted his lunch, and he was wandering up and down the aisles. He looked sad and lonely. I felt, in spite of everything, that Mirta and I owed him a lot. I wanted to cheer him up, so I climbed the moving ladder—which I hadn't used since Enrique had started helping me in the store—to reach the highest shelves. I chose a model kit for him, an imported one of an old-fashioned train. The box said that it had more than a thousand pieces, and, if you added batteries, its lights worked. It was the best model train we had, and it cost a fortune. But Enrique deserved it, and I wanted to give it to him. I climbed down with the gift and called to him from the counter. He was coming back from the farthest shelves, a violet stuffed animal—I think it was a rabbit—hanging from his right hand. Head down, he stopped and looked at me. He looked small among the shelves. I called to him again but he suddenly crouched down, as though startled, and stayed there. It was a strange movement that I didn't understand. I left the train on the counter and approached him slowly to see if something was wrong.

"Enrique, are you all right?"

He was crying, hugging his knees. The rabbit had fallen to one side, facedown on the floor.

"Enrique, I want to give you—"

"I don't want anyone to hit me anymore," he said.

I wondered if something had happened that I hadn't seen—if some customer had given him trouble or if he'd had another fight with a child.

"But Enrique, no one . . ."

I knelt beside him. I wished I had the model train right there; I was sure it would be something special and it hurt me to see him so upset. Mirta would have known what to do, how to soothe him. Then the door to the street opened violently, almost slamming against the wall. Both of us froze. From the floor, we saw, under the shelves, two high heels advancing down the next aisle.

"Enrique!" It was a strong, authoritative voice.

The high heels stopped and Enrique looked at me in fear. He seemed to want to tell me something, and he grabbed my arm.

"Enrique!"

The heels started moving again, this time in our direction, and a woman appeared at the end of the aisle.

"Enrique!" She stormed toward us. "All this time I've been looking for you," she yelled as she stopped very close to him. "Where the hell have you been?"

She slapped him so hard that he lost his balance. Then she grabbed his hand and yanked him up. The woman cursed me, kicked the stuffed rabbit, and practically dragged Enrique away. I followed them for a couple of steps. They passed the counter, headed for the door. When they'd almost reached it, Enrique tripped and fell to the floor. On his knees, he turned to look at me. Then his face crumpled. She grabbed his hand again, yelling, "Enrique, come on!"

I stayed where I was, watching and doing nothing. Just before the door closed, I saw his little fingers trying to pull away from his mother's as she, furious, leaned down to pick him up.

UNDERGROUND

I needed a break, and a drink to clear my head. The road was dark and I still had to drive several more hours. The truck stop was the only one I'd seen for miles. The interior lights gave the place a certain warmth, and there were three cars parked in front. Inside, a young couple was eating hamburgers. There was a guy in the back facing away from me, and another, older man at the bar. I sat down next to him. The things you do when you travel too much, or when it's been such a long time since you've talked to anyone. I ordered a beer. The bartender was fat and slow-moving.

"That'll be five pesos," he said.

I paid and he served me. I'd been dreaming of this beer for hours, and it was a very good one. The old man was staring at the bottom of his drink, or whatever else he might be seeing in the glass.

"He'll tell the story for a beer," said the fat bartender, pointing to the old man.

The old guy seemed to wake up, and he turned toward me. His eyes were light and gray, maybe the beginnings of cataracts or something; he didn't seem to see well. I thought he was going to tease the story a little, or introduce himself. But he stayed quiet, like a blind dog that thinks it's seen something and doesn't have much more to do.

"Come on, buddy," said the fat man, and he winked an eye at me. "Just one beer for gramps."

I said yes, sure. The old man smiled. I took out five more pesos for the fat man, and in less than a minute the old guy's glass was full again. He took a couple of sips and turned automatically toward me. I thought that he must have already told this story a hundred times, and for a moment I regretted sitting down beside him.

"This happened in the interior," he said, pointing at the drying rack, or perhaps toward an imaginary horizon that I couldn't see. "The interior, way out in the country. There was a town

there, a mining town, see? A little town, the mine was just getting going. But there was a plaza, with a church, and the road
that led to the mine was paved. The miners were young. They'd
brought their wives out to the town and after a few years passed
there were already a lot of kids, ya know?"

I nodded. My eyes sought out the fat man, who clearly knew
the story and was occupied with arranging bottles on one side of
the bar.

"Well, those kids spent all day outside. Running from one
house to another, playing. And then it happened that a few of
the kids were playing in an empty lot, and one of them noticed
something strange. The ground there was sort of swollen. It
wasn't much, it wouldn't have caught everyone's attention, but it
seemed like enough to him. Then the others came closer, and
they all made a circle around it and stood like that for a while.
One of them knelt down and started to scratch at the ground
with his hands, and so the others started doing the same. Soon
they found a toy bucket or some other thing that would work as
a shovel, and they started to dig. Other kids joined them over
the course of the afternoon. They showed up and pitched in
without asking questions, as if they'd already heard about the
hole. The first kids got tired and other kids took their places.
But they didn't leave. They stayed nearby, watching the work.
The next day they came back more prepared, with buckets, big
kitchen spoons, gardening trowels, things they had surely asked
their parents for. The hole became a pit. Five or six kids could fit

inside it. Their heads barely rose above it. They loaded the dirt in buckets and passed them up to the kids above, who, in turn, carried it to a mound that was growing bigger and bigger, ya see?"

I nodded, and took advantage of the pause to ask the fat bartender for more beer. I ordered another for the old man, too. He accepted the beer, but didn't seem to like the interruption. He stayed quiet, and went on only after the bartender had placed our new glasses in front of us and turned back to his work.

"The kids started to be interested only in the pit, nothing else could hold their attention. If they couldn't be there digging, they would talk to one another about it, and if they were with adults, they practically didn't talk at all. They obeyed their parents without arguing, without paying attention to what was said, and the only answers heard from them were 'Yes,' 'No,' 'Doesn't matter.' They kept digging. They got more organized about how they worked, taking short shifts. Since the pit was deeper now, they raised the buckets with ropes. In the afternoon, before it got dark, they all pitched in and covered the mouth of the pit with boards. Some of the parents were enthusiastic about the idea of the pit, because they said it was a way for all the kids to play together, and that was good. Others didn't care. There were surely some parents who didn't even know about it. Probably some adult, intrigued, must have gone there at night while the children were asleep, and must have lifted up the boards. But what can you see at night, in an empty pit dug by children? I don't think they found anything. They must have thought it was just a game; that's what they must have thought, right up until the last day."

The guy went back to staring at his glass, and didn't say anything else. I sat there waiting. I wasn't sure if he was finished or not. A few possible comments occurred to me, but none seemed appropriate. I looked for the fat man; he was waiting on the young couple, who were paying. I opened my wallet, counted out five more pesos, and put the money between us. The old man took it and put it in his pocket.

"They lost their children that night. It was starting to get dark. It was the moment of the day when the kids returned home, but there was no sign of them. The adults went out to look for them and they ran into other parents who were also worried, and by the time they started to suspect something had happened, almost all of them were out on the street. They searched haphazardly, individually. They went to the school, to the houses where the kids played. Some parents went as far out as the mine, combing the surroundings, even looking in places the kids couldn't get to on their own. They searched for hours and didn't find a single child. I guess every one of those parents had at some point thought that something bad could happen to their child someday. A kid could climb onto a high wall and fall and crack his skull open in a second. Or one could drown in the reservoir while they played at dunking one another, or get a cherry pit stuck in his throat, or a rock, anything, and die, just like that.

"But what disaster could wipe them all from the face of the earth? The parents argued. They fought. Maybe because they thought they could find some clue, they concentrated on the area around the pit, and then they lifted up the boards. They must have looked at one another in confusion, without understanding what was happening: there was no pit. The boards covered a protuberance, the kind of mound that's left after the earth is disturbed, or when the dead are buried. One might think the pit had caved in, or that the kids had filled it in, but the pile of dirt they had excavated was still there, the adults could see it from where they stood. They went to get shovels and started to dig where the kids had dug before. One mother cried in desperation:

"'Stop, please!' she yelled. 'Slowly, slowly . . . You'll hit them in the head with the shovels.' It took several people to calm her down.

"At first they dug carefully, then more feverishly. But under the ground there was nothing but ground, and some parents gave up and started to leave the pit, confused. Others kept working until the next night, now taking no care, worn out, and in the end they went back to their houses, more alone than ever.

"The governor traveled to the town. He brought supposed specialists to examine the pit. They made the parents repeat the story several times.

"'But where exactly was the pit?' asked the governor.

"'Here, exactly here.'

"'But isn't this the pit you dug?'

"The governor's men walked all over the town, searched some of the houses, and never came back again. Then the madness began. They say that one night a woman heard noises in her house. They were coming from the floor, as if a rat or a mole were digging underneath it. Her husband found her moving the furniture, pulling up the rugs, shouting her son's name while she pounded the floor with her fists. Other parents started to hear the same noises. They moved all the furniture into the corners of their homes. They pulled up the floorboards with their hands. They knocked down basement walls with hammers, dug up their yards, emptied the wells. They filled the dirt streets with holes. They threw things inside, like food, coats, toys, then they covered them over again. They stopped burying their garbage. They dug up their few dead bodies from the cemetery. It's said that some parents kept digging day and night in the empty lot, and that they stopped only when exhaustion or madness finished off their bodies."

The old man looked again at his now empty glass, and I immediately offered him another five pesos. But he had finished; he refused the money.

"Are you leaving?" he asked me. I felt as though it were the first time he had spoken to me. As if the whole story had been no more than that, a paid story that was over now, and for the first time the man's gray, blind eyes were looking at me.

I said yes. I waved to the fat man, who nodded at me from the sink, and we left. Outside, I felt the cold again. I asked if I could give him a ride somewhere.

"No. Thank you, though," he said.

"Would you like a cigarette?"

He stopped. I took out a cigarette and handed it to him. I looked for my lighter in my coat. The fire illuminated his hands. They were dark, thick and rigid like cudgels. I thought his nails could have been those of a prehistoric human. He handed the lighter back to me, and walked away, toward the fields. I watched him move off, without entirely understanding.

"But where are you going?" I asked. "Are you sure you don't want a ride?"

He stopped.

"Do you live here?"

"I work," he said, "out there," and he pointed to the fields.

He hesitated a few seconds, looked at the field, and then he said:

"We're miners."

Suddenly I didn't feel cold anymore. I stayed there a few minutes to watch him walk away. I forced my eyes, searching for some revelatory detail. Only when his figure disappeared completely in the night did I return to the car, turn on the radio, and drive away at full speed.

SLOWING DOWN

Tego made himself some scrambled eggs, but when he sat down at the table and looked at the plate, he found himself unable to eat them.

"What's wrong?" I asked him.

His eyes lingered on the eggs.

"I'm worried," he said. "I think I'm slowing down."

He moved his arm from side to side, slowly, exasperatingly, seemingly on purpose, and he sat looking at me as though waiting for my verdict.

"I don't have the slightest idea what you're talking about," I said. "I'm still too sleepy."

"Didn't you see how long it took me to answer the phone? Or to get to the door, drink a glass of water, brush my teeth . . . ? It's agony."

There was a time when Tego flew through the air at thirty miles an hour. The circus tent was the sky; I dragged the cannon to the center of the ring. The lights hid the audience, but we heard them roar. The velvet curtains opened and Tego appeared in his silver helmet. He raised his arms to receive the applause. His red suit shone above the sand of the ring. I took care of the powder while he climbed up and loaded his thin body into the cannon. The orchestra's drums called for silence, and then it was all in my hands. The only thing you could hear then were the packets of popcorn rustling and the occasional nervous cough. I took the matches from my pocket. I carried them in a silver box that I still have today. A small box, but so bright it could be seen from the highest of the stands. I'd open it, take out a match, and rest it against the sandpaper at the base of the box. At that moment, all eyes were on me. One quick movement and the fire glowed. I lit the fuse. The sound of sparks spread out in every direction. I'd take a few dramatic steps backward to give the impression that something terrible was about to happen—the audience intent on the fuse burning down—and suddenly: *boom*. And Tego, a red and shining arrow, shot out at breakneck speed.

Tego pushed his eggs aside and got up from his chair with effort. He was fat now, and he was old. He breathed with a heavy snort because his spine pressed on I don't know what part of his lungs; he stopped every once in a while to rest, or to think. Sometimes he just sighed and went on. He walked in silence to the kitchen door and stopped.

"I do think I'm slowing down," he said.

He looked at the eggs.

"I think I'm about to die."

I pulled the plate to my side of the table; I knew it would make him furious.

"That's what happens when you can no longer do the thing you know best how to do," he went on. "That's what I was thinking: then you die."

I tasted the eggs, but by then they were cold. It was the last conversation we had; after that he took three stumbling steps toward the living room and fell to the floor, dead.

A journalist from a local paper comes to interview me a few days later. I sign a photograph for the article that shows Tego and me beside the cannon, him in his helmet and red suit, me in blue with the box of matches in my hand. The girl eats it up. She wants to know more about Tego. She asks if I want to say anything special about his death, but I don't feel like talking about it anymore and I can't think of anything to add. Since she doesn't leave, I offer her something to drink.

"Coffee?" I ask.

"Sure!" she says. She seems willing to listen to me for an eternity. But I scratch a match against my silver box to light the flame of the stove, several times, and nothing happens.

ON THE STEPPE

Life on the steppe isn't easy. You're hours away from everything, and there's nothing to look at but a giant tangle of dry shrubs. Our house is several miles from the nearest town, but that's okay: it's comfortable and has everything we need. Pol goes to town three times a week. While he's there he sends off his articles on insects and insecticides to the agricultural magazines, and he does the shopping, following the lists I prepare. During those hours when he's not here, I carry out a series of activities that I prefer to do alone. I don't think Pol would like it if he knew about what I do. But when you're desperate, when you've reached your limit like we have, then the simplest solutions—candles, incense, whatever advice the magazines give—all seem like reasonable options.

There are many fertility recipes and not all of them are trustworthy, so I choose only the most sensible ones and follow the instructions to a T. I have a notebook where I take notes about any relevant detail, any tiny changes I notice in Pol or in me.

It gets dark late on the steppe, which doesn't leave us too much time. We have to have everything ready: the flashlights, the nets. Pol cleans everything while I wait for the time to come. Cleaning off the dust just for it all to get dirty again lends the thing a certain air of ritual, as if before starting out we were already thinking about how to do it better and better, attentively reviewing the routine of recent days to find any detail that could be adjusted, that could lead us to them, or at least to one: ours.

When we're ready, Pol passes me my jacket and scarf and I help him put on gloves, and we both sling backpacks over our shoulders. We go out the back door and walk into the fields. The night is cold, but the wind is calm. Pol goes first, shining the flashlight on the ground. Deeper in, the countryside sinks down a little into long hillocks; we move toward them. Around there the shrubs are small, hardly tall enough to hide our bodies, and Pol thinks that's one of the reasons our plan fails every night. But we keep trying because several times now we thought we saw some, around dawn, when we were already exhausted. In those early-morning hours I'm almost always hiding behind some bush, clutching my net, nodding off and dreaming of things that seem fertile. Pol, on the other hand, turns into a kind of predatory animal. I see him move off, hunched over the plants, and he can stay there, crouching and motionless, for a long time.

I've always wondered what they'll really be like. We've talked about it several times. I think they're the same as the ones in the city, only a little coarser, wilder. Pol, though, is sure they'll be different, and although he's as excited as I am and there's not a single night when the cold and exhaustion convince him to leave the search for another day, when we're out among the bushes, he moves with a certain wariness, as if from one moment to the next something wild could attack him.

Now I'm alone, looking out at the road from the kitchen window. This morning we slept in and then had lunch. Then Pol went to town with the shopping list and his magazine articles. But it's late, he should have been back a while ago and there's still no sign of him. Finally, I see the pickup. As he's pulling up to the house he waves his hand out the window. I go out and help him with the groceries, and he greets me by saying:

"You're not going to believe this."

"What?"

Pol smiles. We carry the bags to the porch and sit in the chairs there.

"So," says Pol, rubbling his hands together. "I met a couple, and they're great."

"Where?"

I ask only to keep him talking, and then he says something wonderful, something I never would have thought of and that nevertheless I realize will change everything.

"They came here for the same reason," he says. His eyes are shining and he knows I'm desperate for him to go on. "And they have one. They've had him a month now."

"They have one? They have one! I can't believe it . . ."

Pol can't stop nodding and rubbing his hands together.

"They invited us over for dinner. Tonight!"

I'm happy to see him happy, and I'm so happy, too—it's as though we'd finally managed it ourselves. We hug and kiss, and right away we start to get ready.

I bake a dessert, and Pol chooses a bottle of wine and his best cigars. While we shower and get dressed, he tells me everything he knows. Arnol and Nabel live some ten miles from here, in a house very much like ours. Pol saw it because they drove back together, in a caravan, until Arnol honked his horn to tell him they were turning and he saw Nabel pointing to the house. "They're great," says Pol again and again, and I feel a little jealous that he already knows so much about them.

"And? What's he like? Did you see him?"

"They leave him at home."

"What do you mean, they leave him at home? Alone?"

Pol shrugs his shoulders. I'm surprised he doesn't think it's odd, but I just ask him for more details while I go on with the preparations.

We close up the house as if we're going away for a long time, then bundle up and go outside. During the drive I carry the apple pie on my lap, taking care it doesn't tilt, and I think about the things I'm going to say, about everything I want to ask Nabel. Maybe when Pol invites Arnol for a cigar they'll leave the two of us alone together. Then maybe I can talk to her about more private things. Maybe Nabel used candles, too; maybe she dreamed often of fertile things, and now that they've gotten one she can tell us exactly what to do.

We honk the horn when we arrive and they come right out to greet us. Arnol is a big guy wearing jeans and a red plaid shirt; he greets Pol with a warm hug, like an old friend he hasn't seen in a long time. Nabel comes out after Arnol and smiles at me. I think we're going to get along. She's also tall, as tall as Arnol but thin, and her clothes are almost the same as his; I regret having dressed up. Inside, the house reminds me of an old mountain lodge. Wooden walls and ceiling, a big fireplace in the living room, and furs on the floor and sofas. It's well lit and heated. It's really not the way I would decorate my house, but I think it's all fine and I return Nabel's smile. There's a delicious smell of sauce and roast meat. It seems Arnol is the chef; he moves around the kitchen shifting dirty dishes around, and he tells Nabel to show us into the living room. We sit on the sofa. She pours wine and brings in a tray of appetizers, and soon Arnol joins us. I want to ask questions right away: How did they catch him, what's he like, what's his name, does he eat well, have they taken him to the doctor yet, is he as cute as the ones from the city? But the conversation lingers on stupid subjects. Arnol asks Pol about insecticides, Pol takes an interest in Arnol's business, then they talk about trucks, the places they buy things; they discover they both argued with the same man, a guy who works in the service station, and they agree he's terrible. Then Arnol excuses himself to go check on the food, Pol offers to help him, and they both leave. I settle into the sofa across from Nabel. I know I should say something friendly before asking her what I want to ask. I compliment her on the house, and then right away I ask:

"Is he cute?"

She blushes and smiles. She looks at me like she's embarrassed, and I feel a knot in my stomach and I'm dying of happiness and I think, *They've got him* and *They've got him and he's beautiful.*

"I'd love to see him," I say. *I want to see him right now*, I think, and I stand up. I look toward the hallway and wait for Nabel to say, *This way.* I'm finally going to see him, hold him.

Then Arnol comes back with the food and calls us to the table.

"Does he sleep all day, then?" I ask, and I laugh as if it were a joke.

"Ana is anxious to meet him," says Pol, and he caresses my hair.

Arnol laughs, but instead of answering he places the serving dish on the table and asks who likes rare meat and who likes it well done, and then we're eating again. Nabel is more talkative during the meal. While the men hold forth on their own subjects, we discover our lives are similar. Nabel asks me for advice about plants and then I get up the nerve to mention the fertility recipes. I bring it up as just a joke, offhand, but Nabel shows interest and I find out she used them, too.

"And the walks? The nighttime hunts?" I say, laughing. "The gloves, the backpacks?"

Nabel is quiet for a second, surprised, and then she starts laughing along with me.

"And the flashlights!" she says, holding her belly. "With those damned batteries that don't last five minutes!"

And me, almost crying:

"And the nets! Pol's net!"

"And Arnol's!" she says. "I just can't tell you!"

Then the men stop talking. Arnol looks at Nabel and he seems surprised. She hasn't noticed yet: she doubles over in an attack of laughter, pounding the table twice with the palm of her hand, and it seems like she's trying to say something else but she can barely breathe. I look at her, amused, and then I look at Pol to make sure he's having a good time, too. Nabel takes a breath, and crying with laughter, says:

"And the shotgun." She pounds the table again. "For God's sake, Arnol! If you'd only stopped shooting! We would have found him much faster . . ."

Arnol looks at Nabel like he wants to kill her, and finally he lets loose with an exaggerated peal of laughter. I look at Pol again, and he's not laughing anymore. Arnol shrugs his shoulders resignedly, seeking a complicit look from Pol. Then he mimes taking aim with a shotgun and shoots. Nabel imitates him. They do it one more time aiming at each other, now a little calmer, until they stop laughing.

"Oh . . . goodness . . ." says Arnol, and he passes the dish around to offer more meat. "Finally, people we can share this whole thing with . . . Anyone want more?"

"So, where is he? We want to see him," Pol finally says.

"You'll see him soon," says Arnol.

"He sleeps a lot," says Nabel.

"All day long."

"So we'll just look at him while he's asleep!" says Pol.

"Oh, no, no," says Arnol. "First, the dessert Ana baked, then a good coffee, and my Nabel here has prepared some games. Do you like strategy games, Pol?"

"But we'd love to see him asleep."

"No," says Arnol. "I mean, it doesn't make sense to see him like that. You can do that any day."

Pol looks at me for a second, then says:

"All right, dessert then."

I help Nabel carry the dishes to the kitchen. I take out the pie that Arnol put in the fridge, I carry it to the table and prepare to serve it. Meanwhile, Nabel is busy in the kitchen with the coffee.

"Where's the bathroom?" asks Pol.

"Oh, the bathroom . . ." says Arnol as he looks toward the kitchen, maybe looking for Nabel. "It's just that it's not working so well, and . . ."

Pol makes a gesture to indicate it doesn't matter.

"Where is it?"

Maybe without meaning to, Arnol looks toward the hallway. Then Pol gets up and starts to walk and Arnol gets up, too.

"I'll go with you."

"That's okay, it's not necessary," says Pol, already in the hallway.

Arnol follows him a few steps.

"To your right," he says. "The bathroom is the one on the right."

My eyes follow Pol until he finally enters the bathroom. Arnol stands a few seconds with his back to me, looking toward the hallway.

"Arnol," I say, and it's the first time I've called him by his name. "Pie?"

"Sure," he says. He looks at me and then turns back to the hallway.

"Ready," I say, and I push the first plate toward his chair. "Don't worry, he'll be a while."

I smile at him, but he doesn't respond. He comes back to the table and sits in his chair with his back to the hall. He seems uncomfortable, but in the end he picks up his fork and cuts off an enormous portion of pie that he puts in his mouth. I look at him, a little surprised, and go on serving. From the kitchen, Nabel asks how we like our coffee. I'm about to answer when I see Pol come silently out of the bathroom and cross the hall into another room. Arnol looks at me, waiting for an answer. I tell Nabel that we love coffee, we like it any which way. The light in the other room goes on and I hear a muffled sound, like something heavy falling on a carpet. Arnol is going to turn toward the hallway, so I say his name:

"Arnol." He looks at me, but starts to stand up.

I hear another sound, then Pol screams and something falls to the floor—a chair, maybe—then a heavy piece of furniture is moved, things break. Arnol runs toward the hallway and takes down the rifle that's hanging on the wall. I get up to run after him; Pol comes backing out of the room, keeping his eyes on what's inside. Arnol goes right for him but Pol reacts, hits the rifle out of his hands, then pushes him aside and runs to me.

I can't figure out what's happening, but I let him take me by the arm and we run out. I hear the door slowly closing behind us as we run, and then a crash as it's slammed back open. Nabel is screaming. Pol gets into the pickup and starts it, and I get in on the passenger side. We back out of the driveway, and for a few seconds the headlights shine onto Arnol as he runs toward us.

Once we're on the road we drive awhile in silence, trying to calm down. Pol's shirt is torn—he almost lost the whole right sleeve—and he has some deep scratches on his arm that are oozing blood. Soon we approach our house at top speed, and at top speed we pass it and leave it behind. I touch his arm, about to stop him, but he's breathing hard, with his tense hands clutching the steering wheel. He scans the black expanse to either side, and behind us in the rearview mirror. We should slow down. We could die if an animal crossed in front of us. Then I think that one of *them* could also cross—and it could be ours. But Pol speeds up even more, as if, in the terror his frenzied eyes belie, he were counting on precisely that.

A GREAT EFFORT

He and his father were a yellow animal, a single animal looking at itself in the mirror. It was a recurring dream. He woke up anxious, and every time he had it, it was harder to fall back asleep. During the day he felt stiffer than usual, more hunched over. His wife even asked him once if he was all right, though when he tried to explain, she seemed not to want to know too much. Then someone gave him Mrs. Linn's name. He could go to her or some other woman; there was one in every neighborhood. The important thing, his friend told him while writing the phone number on a piece of paper, was not to let it go on.

He went to see her, and after that he returned once a week. The relief after each session helped him define his distress: his nervousness disappeared, and so did the anxiety that pulled his throat toward his stomach. The effect lasted all that day—a fullness that, according to him, was comparable to walking on air—and there was a residual peace that lasted for a few days after that. But in the end, the stiffness always came back.

In the fifth session he described the dream, and Mrs. Linn applied lavender essential oils and opened the window all the way. He sunk his head into the massage table's generous opening and let Mrs. Linn work. Her hands, elbows, and knees were that woman's true strength, and he let himself be influenced by them.

In the sixth session he talked about his father, about that first time his father had left home, and about the police officer, a woman, who called to let them know. He'd been found walking alone on the highway median; a driver had called 911 right away. He remembers his mother on the phone and the officer's voice scolding her: "Do you realize he was putting everyone in danger, wandering alone along the highway like that?" Someone had to go pick him up from the station.

His mother put on her jacket over her pajamas, and he and his sister sat on the living room sofa and waited. "If you move your butts from that sofa," their mother told them, "no more Dad for anyone."

When the session ended, Mrs. Linn would say, "Open your eyes slowly." It was pleasant to find the light a little more tenuous, and he wasn't disturbed at not knowing when exactly she'd closed the curtains. In the eighth session he told about the next time his father had tried to leave them: his mother was making the shopping list, and his father was looking attentively at the tiles in the kitchen, the yellow ones.

"I know it's strange," he clarified for Mrs. Linn, "but I'm sure he was only looking at the yellow ones. Yellow like in my dream."

He was afraid that among so many patients Mrs. Linn would forget the smallest details, and maybe it was there, in the yellow, where the important point lay. But Mrs. Linn's fingers moved quickly up his back, and he understood how familiar she was with this kind of story, and he trusted that he had to go ahead with his own, without so many explanations.

"My father got up and left the kitchen," he went on, "and it was the way he did it, a little stiffer than usual, that put me on alert. 'Where are you going?' my mother asked him. 'You're leaving without the shopping list.' It was fairly violent, the way she stuffed the paper into his fist, like cramming an oversize letter into the mouth of a too-soft mailbox. But my mother knew what she was doing: with an order in his hands, my father would have to return."

"Inhale and exhale deeply," Mrs. Linn reminded him. "If you like, you can close your eyes."

Sometimes he raised his head from the opening in the massage table to add a detail or size up Mrs. Linn's eyes. But she dug her elbow into some strategic point of his body and put him right back in his place. Her elbows, her fists and knees approached, always shining and moist, avid. She shook the tubes of lotion before opening and squeezing them. She said it was good for the lotion to feel cold on first contact with the body, because it stimulated the epidermis and activated the muscles.

"I'm afraid," he said in the ninth session, "afraid of a lot of things."

He was immediately ashamed. He'd spoken without thinking; maybe the contact with the massage table put him too much at ease.

"Relax your arms," said Mrs. Linn.

Maybe something had softened more than it should, and now there were things he could no longer control.

"Open your fists."

Mrs. Linn poured more oil on her hands and extended her fingers several times, as if doing some sort of stretching exercise.

He felt more docile than usual; he was on the verge of tears, and it was a very embarrassing thing. But he took a deep breath and steeled himself to go on.

His father came back at midnight, almost twelve hours later and in the pouring rain, carrying the purchases in two large, drenched bags. In his last years of grade school, the father's looming disappearances tormented him more and more, and not only because of the pain of feeling abandoned. It was resentment. Resentment that inflated in his chest and was caused by his father, so clumsy and weak and unable to leave for good. It was a painful ball of air that he carried with him, always with his mouth closed. Because if the father ever did manage to leave, that ball of air would be all that remained of him, and he wasn't willing to let go of it so easily.

In the tenth session, Mrs. Linn asked about the dream again. He still had it, although the treatment was relieving the symptoms. He and his father were still a yellow animal, a single animal looking at itself in the mirror.

In the twelfth session he again felt the need to make some clarifications. His parents didn't get along badly, that didn't seem to be the problem, and neither were there financial problems. Sometimes these explanations were for himself, but he still made them out loud in order to include Mrs. Linn. Whatever it was that happened there on the massage table, it was a joint task. He said what he had to say, and, in exchange, Mrs. Linn's elbows sank in on either side of his shoulder blades, they stabbed inward and outward, they acknowledged and permeated. There were only one or two occasions when, out of pure exhaustion, he didn't say anything about his father in the whole session. And Mrs. Linn kneaded him more gently, pinching him in the lumbar zones a few times, emotionless.

A few months after high school started, the father left again. And one afternoon, finally, the father managed not to come back. For a time he was on the lookout, expecting the police to find him again. Would his father have some document with his address on him? His mother quickly got used to living without her husband. Almost three years later, the phone rang and it was his father. "I feel very alone," his voice said.

"Where are you, Dad? I'll come get you," he said, and when there was only silence, he tried: "Are you to the west? Or should I take the highway? Are you near or far?" He waited, but the father had already hung up.

"Does it hurt there?" Mrs. Linn asked sometimes, and her hands moved around the painful zones.

But, and maybe it was better this way, she almost never asked the question when it really did hurt.

Later on, his sister left home, and he did the same a few years after. He left on a Saturday; he remembers because his father came home on a Wednesday. He had waited for his father nearly seven years, but all it took was for him to pack his own suitcases and leave home, and his father, just four days later, rang the doorbell of the house. His mother says that she looked out and saw him waving at her from the gate, and that for some days after, she didn't quite know what to do with him. They agreed to sleep in separate rooms, and soon they grew used to each other again.

When his son was born, the past became distant for all of them. They had Sunday dinners with the family and his father tousled the grandson's hair with such affection that he wondered if he hadn't exaggerated the pain his father had caused him. When it came down to it, he thought, maybe that's what adolescence was all about: the invention of a couple of unforgivable events that help you leave home. And that's the way things still were with them.

A few weeks ago, he went to see Mrs. Linn without an appointment. He had his father in the passenger seat, in hermetic silence. He needed to see her, and she understood that as soon as she heard that both of them were in the waiting room. She wasted no time ushering him in, while his father waited outside.

Mrs. Linn asked him to sit on the massage table and tell her what had happened. He said that that afternoon he'd been reading in the kitchen when his son came to get him and dragged him to his room. He'd prepared a little puppet show, and asked his father to sit and watch it. His son went behind an improvised curtain, and he could catch glimpses of the boy as he made a great effort to put the puppet show on well. He had never seen his son so serious. And now Mrs. Linn had to be patient, because what happened was something strange, difficult to explain.

Mrs. Linn nodded, but she reached toward her tubes of lotion and picked one up before sitting down beside the massage table.

The boy brought a puppet out onto the stage and the puppet opened its mouth, white and huge, and it trembled without closing it, as if it were screaming. He was only a few feet away, as alarmed as the puppet. But what happened next, what happened next was impossible to explain to Mrs. Linn. The boy hid the puppet behind the curtain and brought it out again, made it scream again, and hid it again. His son did that over and over, until he recognized the pain between the nape of his neck and his throat. The pain that stiffened him and terrified him in his dreams, the pain that tied him to his father and to his own image in the mirror, the yellow pain.

Mrs. Linn held her largest tube of lotion, and she accidentally squeezed it too hard. The almond perfume flooded the room.

"I felt," he said, trying to understand himself, "my son's boundless need for attention. An insatiable need, that's what I felt. A need impossible to satisfy."

Mrs. Linn put down the tube of lotion and nervously extended her fingers, as though stretching them.

"And then I couldn't look at him, at my son. I looked away." He tried to concentrate, but he felt a little dizzy.

Then the boy put down the puppet and he looked out from the stage himself. He hid behind the curtain for a few seconds and then appeared again. The pain he felt every time his son disappeared was something brutal. Every time the boy hid behind the curtain again, an invisible thread pulled at him violently.

Mrs. Linn brought the tube of lotion to her chest, and for a moment her elbows poked out behind her, more ready than ever to sink and compress.

"I understood that I could no longer live with him, or

without him. It was a huge mistake, whatever it was that joined us. A tragedy in which we would both fail miserably."

Mrs. Linn handed him the tube of lotion and he held it, and somehow the tube gave him the strength to go on.

He tried to explain himself: he couldn't meet the boy's gaze. He looked for a point among the toys in the room, a fixed point that would save him from the panic, and he latched on to a yellow puppet hanging near the window.

Mrs. Linn's arms now hung straight down from her shoulders and her fingers were just barely moving, as if they were practicing in the air a new way to knead.

"So I went to get my father, and I made him get into the car. I got on the highway and drove in silence for about thirty miles."

For a few seconds Mrs. Linn's fingers stopped, as if they'd lost the thread or didn't entirely understand what he had just said, but as soon as he went on, Mrs. Linn's fingers followed him.

His father didn't say anything as they drove, and when the city's lights started to disappear, he stopped the car on the side of the road and asked his father to get out.

"I couldn't leave home. I'm as weak as my father was. But there *is* something I could do, something that could change things in the long term."

He could give his father the push that he'd needed his whole life in order to leave them. He could forgive him and give him permission. He could sacrifice himself and disrupt this tragic cycle: loosen a link in the chain to break the circle. Maybe that way he would free his own son from the pain of sons, and his son's children from the same pain.

Mrs. Linn leaned over toward her shelf and quickly exchanged the tube of lotion.

He got out of the car and turned around to open his father's door. What he felt at that moment was the complete opposite of fear—it was something close to madness, but with the absolute certainty he was taking the right step. The exciting anguish of recognizing that what one is doing will ultimately change something important. To free his father was to free them all. His father had always known he had to leave. Now his son was there to help him. But the father didn't move.

"He didn't move," he said. "I told him to get out. I waited. I said it again, harshly. But he couldn't even look me in the eyes."

He'd only sunk into his seat, terrified.

"Where is your father?" asked Mrs. Linn. "Bring him in." He looked at her, he looked at his Mrs. Linn. He hesitated a moment, trying to emerge from his story's aura, and a gentle push on his shoulder set him in motion.

"Go on, get him."

When he came back with his father, Mrs. Linn had turned on her two lavender vaporizers. She circled the father and the son a few times, as if she needed to be sure they were similar enough. Then she had the father sit on the massage table. Perhaps the father thought he was dealing with something else, because before he gave himself over completely and let the specialist work, he made his son promise not to say a word to his mother. His son assured him he would not, and he had to explain that his face went into the opening, and that it wasn't anything painful.

Mrs. Linn indicated that he, on the other hand, should wait seated in the armchair beside the table. But he was restless and didn't sit down, and before he knew it, Mrs. Linn's elbows, fists, and knees climbed up his father like a big spider in a trance. They sank and spun over his shoulders, his shoulder blades, his spine and coccyx. Her fists compressed the waist, then lifted it and dropped it. His father's entire body let itself be kneaded and resettled. On the table, Mrs. Linn held him by the shoulders, arching him back more than he would have thought a father could arch. There were tugs, pushes, rotations. The oiled elbows sank into the hips and he, never taking his eyes from the father, let his body fall, completely relaxed, into the armchair. As if Mrs. Linn had been waiting for exactly that moment, she dug one of her knees into his father's spine. It was a quick and surgical movement. Something cracked in his body, so loudly he felt it in his own, so loudly that he was frightened by the tug, the precise and expert correction. The three of them were still for a few seconds. Then, with relief, he understood it was all a good sign.

Mrs. Linn said goodbye to them in the waiting room. The receptionist made a file for his father and handed him a card.

They walked to the car and made the trip back in silence.

They passed the plaza, and at the stoplight to cross the avenue, they both sat looking at the pedestrian crosswalk. There were green, red, and yellow lights. There was a turnoff for each street, and at each corner everyone knew what to do. He waited for his signal, and his father accepted the wait. When the light changed to green, they were already feeling much better.

THE HEAVY SUITCASE OF BENAVIDES

He returns to the room carrying a suitcase. Durable, lined in brown leather, it stands on four wheels and offers up its handle elegantly at knee level. He doesn't regret his actions. He thinks that the stabbing of his wife had been fair, but he also knows that few people would understand his reasons. And that's why he opts for the following plan: Wrap the body in garbage bags to keep the blood from seeping. Open the suitcase next to the bed and take every pain required to bend the body of a woman dead after twenty-nine years of marriage, and push it toward the floor so it falls into the suitcase. Unaffectionately cram the extra flesh into the free space, finally getting the body to fit. Once that's done, more out of diligence than caution, gather the bloody sheets and put them into the washing machine. Swaddled in leather atop four now buckling wheels, the woman's weight doesn't diminish in the slightest, and though Benavides is small, he has to lean down a little to reach the handle, a gesture that lends neither grace nor efficiency to his task. But Benavides is an organized man, and within a few hours he's out on the street, at night, taking short steps and pulling the suitcase behind him, walking toward Dr. Corrales's house.

Dr. Corrales lives nearby. There's a large, plant-covered gate above which loom the residence's upper floors; Benavides rings the doorbell. A feminine voice on the intercom says, "Hello?" And Benavides says, "It's Benavides, I need to talk to Dr. Corrales." The intercom crackles like it's on its last legs, then falls silent. Standing on tiptoe, Benavides peers between the lush plants growing on the other side of the brick wall, but he can't see anything. He rings the doorbell again. The voice on the intercom says, "Hello?" And Benavides says, again, "It's Benavides, I want to talk to Dr. Corrales."

The device makes the same noises and is silent again. Benavides, perhaps tired out by the tensions of the day, lays the suitcase on the ground and sits down on it. A while later, the gate opens and some men emerge, saying their goodbyes. Benavides stands up and looks at the men, but doesn't see Dr. Corrales among them.

"I need to speak to Dr. Corrales," says Benavides.

One of the men asks his name.

"Benavides."

The man tells him to wait a moment and goes back inside the house. The rest of the men look at Benavides curiously. Some minutes later, the man who had gone inside returns:

"The doctor is waiting for you," he tells Benavides, and Benavides takes hold of his suitcase and enters the house with the man.

It's no surprise to find Dr. Corrales in the midst of displaying his talents before a dozen of his disciples. Sitting upright at the piano, surrounded by young and beautiful admirers, he gives himself over to a sonata that grows more demanding by the second. Benavides waits among the columns in the center of the hall until the performance ends, and the men who had surrounded Dr. Corrales applaud and open up the semicircle they had formed around him. Dr. Corrales gratefully accepts the glass of champagne he is offered. A man approaches the doctor and whispers something in his ear, looking over at Benavides. Corrales smiles and motions Benavides over. Benavides and his suitcase approach.

"How are you, Benavides . . . ?"

"Doctor, I need to speak with you in private."

"Tell me, Benavides, we're all friends here . . ."

"Telling you is no problem, Doctor. The thing is that . . ." Benavides looks at his suitcase. "It's that I need to show you something."

Dr. Corrales lights a cigarette and studies the suitcase.

"All right, no matter. I'll give you five minutes, Benavides. Come with me to my study."

The white marble stairs are hard for Benavides, who bears the inconvenience of that oversize suitcase. The next staircase, which starts on the second floor, is worse still. It's too narrow, with high, short steps framed by dark corridor walls papered in brown, black, and wine-colored arabesques, and it makes Benavides's efforts into an exaggerated struggle. Dragging the heavy suitcase step by step, he is soon drenched in sweat, while Dr. Corrales's agile and unhampered body bounds away and disappears up the stairs. And perhaps it's the damp, dark solitude in which Benavides finds himself that makes him reflect on and doubt the present. Not the immediate present—that is, the present of the stairs, the effort, and the sweat—but that of the murder. Maybe this is when he tells himself it could all be a dream, that he's been fantasizing again about killing his wife. He wonders if he is now climbing the stairs to his doctor's study—the doctor he has imposed upon at two-thirty in the morning, taking him away from his famous and prestigious guests—only to have to tell him, *Look, Doctor, I'm sorry, but this has all been a mistake*. What to do, then? It would be senseless to lie and useless to run back down the stairs, given that in his next session with the doctor he would have to tell the truth anyway, and he'd also have to come up with some excuse that would justify fleeing in the wee morning hours with a heavy suitcase in tow.

At the top of the stairs Benavides finds Dr. Corrales waiting by the small door to his study, waving him in. Once inside, the doctor turns on a small lamp; its tenuous light barely illuminates the space around them. He motions Benavides to a chair on the other side of the desk. Without letting go of the suitcase handle, Benavides obeys. The doctor puts on a pair of glasses and searches in his file cabinet for the last name Benavides.

"Very well, why are we in such a hurry to move your next session up thirty-eight hours?"

Benavides shifts in his seat.

"Doctor, this is all a big misunderstanding, I owe you an apology. You see . . ."

Dr. Corrales observes Benavides over his eyeglasses.

"It's a dream. I mean . . . I'm confused, for a moment I thought I had killed my wife and stuffed her into this suitcase, and now I understand that really—"

Dr. Corrales interrupts him:

"Let's see if I understand, Benavides . . . You barge into my house at two-thirty in the morning while I'm having an intimate party, with a suitcase you say holds your wife, murdered and stuffed inside, and now you're trying to convince me that it's all a dream so you can get up and leave, just like that . . ."

Benavides clutches the handle.

"You think I'm stupid, Benavides."

"No, Doctor."

Dr. Corrales looks at him for a moment. A few seconds at him, a few seconds at his suitcase. He doesn't seem to be annoyed or put out. It rather seems that, somewhere deep inside him, he has already made some kind of decision.

"Stand up!"

"Yes, Doctor."

Benavides stands up without letting go of the handle, a hindrance that makes him lean slightly to his right.

"You, sir, are highly upset. Exhausted. We're going to try to calm down, okay?"

"Yes, Doctor."

"Leave your wife here and follow me."

"My wife?"

"Didn't you say that was your wife?"

Corrales is already heading for the door, but Benavides is unable to let go of the suitcase handle.

"Relax, Benavides. You're overexcited. You need rest. I'll give you a room, you can sleep for a bit, and in the meantime I'll think about what we'll do. How does that sound?"

"No, Doctor, I'd rather . . ."

Corrales pushes a glass of water toward Benavides. He gives him two white pills.

"This will help you," he says, and he watches until Benavides obeys and swallows them.

He urges Benavides to leave the study without the suitcase.

"We'll come back for her later," says Corrales.

They walk down a carpeted hallway along which every few feet there are two doors across from each other. Corrales stops before the third set of doors and opens the one on the right.

"Your room," he announces. "Rest while I take care of your problem."

Benavides wakes up in the light of a new day, and for a moment he believes himself to be in his own bed, beside his wife, on an ordinary unhappy morning. Quickly, he realizes his situation.

What to do with his wretchedness? To think that just a few rooms away his wife awaits him stuffed inside a suitcase. He is sure he will hear the doctor's voice on the other side of the door: *Wake up, Benavides, your problem is solved*, or *Good morning, Benavides, I'm here with your wife and she's feeling better now*, or simply *Wake up, Benavides, it was all a bad dream, let's have some breakfast while we wait for your taxi*. It's the problem's prompt resolution that matters here, not the manner by which it is solved.

But time passes and nothing happens. Every object is composed of millions of shifting particles, and yet Benavides cannot perceive anything in the room that could be considered movement. Finally, he stands up. He's slept in his clothes, so now he only has to put on his shoes. He opens the door. His eyes hurt from the light coming in the windows at the end of the hallway. He isn't sure which of the many doors leads to the room where he left his wife the night before.

He finds the study, and matters get worse. What it holds, or more like what it doesn't hold, is distressing. Inside the room, nothing that resembles a suitcase. And the wretchedness finds Benavides even in a house that isn't his: someone has taken his wife. Walking quickly, he searches the second floor, goes down the stairs, crosses the central hall toward more corridors, enters parts of the house heretofore unknown to him: there are even more hallways, other rooms, winter gardens distributed capriciously throughout the massive house, and a large kitchen into which he bursts, exhausted, only to have three meticulously uniformed cooks look at him for a few seconds, their faces betraying no surprise. But Dr. Corrales is nowhere to be found, and Benavides does not see his suitcase or any other, and he certainly does not find his wife up walking and talking. The women in the kitchen return to their culinary tasks.

"I'm looking for Dr. Corrales."

"He's having breakfast," says one of the women.

Benavides looks back for a moment toward the empty hallways, then turns back to the kitchen.

"Where?"

"He's having breakfast," repeats the woman. "We don't know where."

Benavides turns back to the hallway. Dr. Corrales is there behind him, holding a steaming cup of coffee and a half-finished piece of cheese bread.

"You arrived last night in very poor condition, Benavides. A lot of alcohol. I stored your suitcase in the garage. Shall I call a car for you?"

"You don't understand. There was an incident last night, a problem, at my house, you see . . ."

"I understand, Benavides. You know that you don't have to explain anything here, you just take it easy and be on your way," says Corrales, offering a piece of cheese bread to Benavides.

"No, thank you," says Benavides. "It's about my wife."

"Yes, I know, it's almost always about that, but what can we do . . ."

"No, you don't understand, my wife is dead."

"Why do you keep repeating that, Benavides? I tell you, I do understand . . . Mine has been dead since the day we got married. Every once in a while she speaks: she insists that I'm fat, that we have to do something about my mother, and then there's the matter of the environment . . . but you mustn't concern yourself with them . . ."

"No, look, give me my suitcase and I'll show you."

"In the garage, Benavides. I'll leave you to it now because I have patients waiting."

"No, listen . . ."

"Go home: have yourself a shower, and before you go to bed, take these pills for me, and you'll just see how well you sleep."

Benavides refuses the pills.

"Come with me, I beg you. I need to show you what I have in the suitcase."

Corrales finishes his bread. He sighs and nods, looking at his empty mug.

They go out the front door and cross the garden. As they walk, a tingling feeling intensifies Benavides's nerves. They enter through the front of the garage. Inside, it's dark. Corrales turns on the light and everything is illuminated: tool benches, boxes of old files, broken appliances, and the suitcase, alone and upright in the middle of the garage.

"Show me, Benavides."

Benavides walks over to the suitcase and rolls it slowly. He moves it with the intention of laying it down; he has the hope he will feel the light weight of an empty valise. Then it would all be a mistake, as Corrales himself explained last night when Benavides had shown up—drunk, as Corrales said just now. *I'm sorry, Corrales, I swear this won't happen again,* he will have to say. Or maybe, on opening the suitcase and finding it empty, his eyes would meet Corrales's complicit gaze; maybe Corrales would say, *It's over, Benavides, you don't owe me anything.* But when he takes the handle, the weight of a body much like his wife's reminds him that actions have consequences. His face goes pale, he feels weak, and the suitcase falls onto its side with a thud and stains the floor with a dark, thick liquid.

"Do you feel all right, Benavides?"

Benavides replies, "Yes, of course." He can't think of anything but the twisted-up body. The suitcase gives off a smell of putrefaction.

"What's in it, Benavides?"

Then Benavides discovers his error: trusting Dr. Corrales, having faith in the doctor. As if a man dedicated to health in life could ever contend with death. So he says, "Nothing."

"What do you mean, 'nothing'?"

"I mean, don't worry about it. You go see your patients now and I'll manage here."

"Is this a joke?"

Corrales approaches. Benavides bends down and holds on to the buckles so Corrales can't open them, but the doctor kneels down next to him and says, "Let me see, come now, move." And with a simple shove, Benavides falls over. Corrales struggles with the buckles but can't open them: pushed to their limit by the suitcase's excess load, they resist.

"Help me," orders Corrales.

"No, look here . . ."

"I'm telling you to help me, Benavides. Stop this nonsense," says Corrales, indicating Benavides should sit on the suitcase. Benavides finds the most opportune spot on the irregular leather surface, and puts the weight of his body on top of his wife's. Corrales is strong, and together they finally manage to un-buckle the clasps.

Benavides stands up and moves away from the suitcase that, though now unbuckled, has still not been opened. He doesn't want to see. Rapid pulses squeeze his heart. Corrales studies the scene. *He knows*, thinks Benavides when he sees the doctor stand up and walk toward him. Corrales stops beside him and looks at the suitcase. In a low voice, almost hypnotized, he or-ders Benavides:

"Open it."

Benavides stays where he is. Maybe he thinks that this is the end, or maybe he's not thinking about anything, but ultimately he obeys and walks over to the suitcase. When he opens it, he forgets Corrales for a moment: his wife is curled up like a fetus, her head bent inward, her knees and elbows forced into the rigid, leather-lined box, her fat filling up all the empty space. *What a thing, nostalgia,* Benavides says to himself. *All those years just to see her like this.*

Threads of blood trickle toward him over the floor. Corra-les's voice returns him to reality:

"Benavides . . ." And the doctor's cracked voice betrays his anguish.

"Benavides . . ." Corrales, walking slowly, approaches the suitcase without taking his eyes from its contents. His eyes, full of tears, finally turn to meet Benavides's gaze. "Benavides . . . This is drastic. It's . . . It's . . . wonderful," he concludes.

Benavides, dubious, stays silent. He looks back at the suitcase but what he sees is what is there: his wife, purple, coiled like a worm in tomato sauce.

"Wonderful," repeats Corrales, shaking his head. He looks at the suitcase for a moment, then at Benavides, as if he can't understand how Benavides has been able to do such a thing for himself. "You are a genius. And to think that I underestimated you, Benavides. A genius. Let's see. Let me clear my head—it's no small thing you're proposing with this . . ." He rests his arm around Benavides's shoulders with friendly enthusiasm. "Well, let me offer you a drink. Believe it or not, I know just the person you need."

Corrales lets go of Benavides and heads toward the garage exit.

"Genius, truly beautiful," he repeats in a low voice as he walks away. Benavides takes a moment to react, but as soon as he understands that he's about to be left alone, he looks at his suitcase one last time and runs after the doctor.

Olives, sliced cheese and salami, potato chips, little cheese-flavored crackers, onion and ham. Everything neatly arranged on a large wooden tray on the coffee table in the main living room, along with three fine crystal glasses into which Corrales pours white wine.

"Donorio, this is my friend Benavides, the man I've told you so much about."

Donorio curiously studies Benavides's small body and finally puts out his hand. Corrales smiles, pours more wine, and invites the men to eat something.

"Donorio, you have no idea what you're about to see," says Corrales. "Now, I don't want to sound arrogant, I know you have experience with great artists. But even so, I don't think you can imagine what we've got prepared for you. Isn't that right, Benavides?"

Benavides finishes off his wine in one gulp.

"I want to see it," says Donorio.

They cross in the night from the house to the garage. Corrales goes first, enjoying the slow walk toward success; Donorio follows, distrustful but curious. Finally, lagging, sensing the suitcase nearby, Benavides feels his fragile nerves gather into large and fibrous knots.

Corrales has the men enter in darkness, since he prefers the impact the sudden image will have when he turns on the light.

"Benavides, guide Donorio to you-know-what and let me know when he's ready."

Benavides stops in the center of the garage. Feeling his way in the darkness, guided by the sounds, Donorio comments:

"There's a strange smell . . . as though of . . ."

"Here comes the light," says Corrales, and in effect, with the tips of Benavides's and Donorio's shoes nearly touching the pool of thick blood, it appears in front of them, horrible, defiant, authentically innovative: the work.

What is violence if not this very thing we are witness to now? thinks Donorio, and a shiver runs from his legs to the nape of his neck. Violence reproduced before his eyes in its most primitive form. Savage. He could touch it, smell it. It was fresh and intact and awaiting a response from its viewers.

Corrales joins them.

"This is going to go over well," says Donorio.

Corrales nods. Beside them, Benavides's small body trembles. His weak voice speaks for the first time in Donorio's presence.

"You don't understand," he manages to say.

"How could we not, Benavides?" says Corrales.

"It's extraordinary!" says Donorio. "Horror and beauty! What a combination . . ."

"Horror, yes, but . . ." Benavides stammers, looking at his wife. "I mean that . . ."

"You're going to be rich, famous! There is zero competition with a work like this one. The public will fall at your feet."

"Trust him, Benavides, Donorio is the best there is."

"Oh, no, Benavides here is the best," concludes Donorio. "I'm just a curator, my part is minimal. The important thing here is the work, *Violence*, understand?"

"My wife."

"No, Benavides, believe me, I know marketing and that won't work. The title is *Violence*."

A new anguish, uncontrollable. And Benavides confesses:

"I killed her. I killed her . . . then I just wanted to hide her."

Corrales gives Benavides a few affectionate pats on the back, but his attention is directed purely and exclusively at Donorio's instructions.

"It'll be best if we conserve it in a cold environment. Do you have air-conditioning in the garage?"

"Yes, yes, of course."

"I killed her!" Benavides falls to his knees.

"Good, then let's start by refrigerating the place. I'm going to make a couple of calls." Donorio takes a few steps toward the door but soon he stops and turns toward Corrales, full of sincerity. Benavides's wailing obliges him to raise his voice: "I'm grateful to you for thinking of me. This is a big opportunity."

"Me, I killed her, like this . . ." Benavides pounds his closed fists on the floor. "I killed her like this."

"Donorio, ask for the phone and take care of what you need to do," says Corrales as he walks the curator to the door.

"Like this, I killed her like this."

Benavides drags himself over the floor in no particular direction, pounding against the floor whatever objects he finds. "Like that, like that!"

"Don't amuse yourself here, Corrales," says Donorio, already in the doorway. "There will be time later for contemplation and delight."

"I understand perfectly. You go on and we'll catch up with you."

Donorio nods and goes out into the garden. When Corrales turns, a now listless Benavides is pounding on his wife's body.

"I did it. Me," Benavides mutters. Corrales stops him.

"Leave her be, Benavides! She's perfect like that, don't ruin her."

"But I killed her . . ."

"Yes, Benavides, yes. We know it was you, no one is going to take that away from you," says Corrales as he helps Benavides stand up. He adds: "Trust us with this, you'll just see how you take your place among the stars."

"The sky?" asks Benavides. "With my wife?"

He feels that something is wrong in his head, there's something he can't manage to understand, and his body falls, collapsing beside the suitcase.

In the light of a new day, Benavides wakes up and opens his eyes. For a moment he believes he is in his own bed, beside his wife, on a normal unhappy morning. But soon he remembers the truth and sits up. Where is his wife now? In the garage? Still in the suitcase? Has Donorio taken her? Corrales? He leaves the room. He's been wearing the same clothes for two days now, and in the hallway's harsh light he can see that parts of his clothes are taking on a grayish hue. Although he estimates he has slept for a prudent number of hours, he has not rested. He feels exhausted, and he realizes that once again he must scour the rooms in search of Dr. Corrales. After some time, once he has checked the study, the first-floor rooms, the entrance hall, the living room, the hallways around the winter gardens, Benavides—fortuitously, as on the previous day—comes across the kitchen and asks the women:

"Corrales?"

They reply in the negative.

This time Benavides will not go looking for him. Some men wait apathetically for others to command them. But he will solve this on his own, and at once. He will call a taxi and take his wife home. He's already leaving the house and crossing the garden. Halfway to the garage he stops: in front of its open doors he sees a dozen men dressed in blue rushing about. On their backs gleams a logo printed on a white rectangle: "Museum of Modern Art. Installation and Transportation." Benavides realizes that the garage has been entirely emptied out. That is, all the furniture, every item or object that once formed part of the household landscape, has been removed, and now, in a larger, empty space, alone, unique, original, sits the work. And there are Corrales and Donorio, attentive, cordial, open to the artist's feelings:

"How did you sleep, Benavides?"

"That's my wife."

Corrales looks at Donorio, and in his voice is the slow melody of growing disappointment.

"I told you, Donorio, this kind of site-specific exhibit is not to the artist's liking. We should have brought the work to the museum."

"My wife."

"I've been working in this field for years, Corrales. Believe me, the public will prefer it this way."

"But she's my wife."

"But, Benavides, you are not an artist for the common man. Your work is directed at a select audience of intellectuals, minds that scorn even the innovations of the museum, men who appreciate something more, above and beyond the simple work. That is . . ."

Donorio's arm gestures in a flourish toward the garage, while Benavides and Corrales await his conclusion.

"Context," Donorio finishes.

"Beautiful, quite so . . . How absurd to question his strategy," says Corrales.

"But she's my wife," Benavides repeats.

"Benavides, please, this subject has already been discussed.

The subject is not 'the wife,' it's 'violence' . . . Let's not go back over this, I beg you. We've agreed," he sighs. "As I was saying: context. In any case, we're going to add certain elements. Getting out of the museum is a novel way to go, but we must maintain standards, the right environment."

"Yes, of course . . ." says Corrales.

Benavides repeats once more what he has already said over and over. He moves away from the men and approaches the suitcase. Donorio signals to the men in blue; Benavides makes a break for it. Someone shouts, "Don't let him touch it!" and everyone stops what they're doing to run after Benavides's short steps, and he barely manages to touch the suitcase's handle before a dozen heavy blue bodies pile on top of him. What a disgrace, his disgrace; in the darkness of other men's weight, he concludes that death must be something like this. From far away, Donorio's voice reaches him: precise instructions to be executed upon his own person. And that is the end of his short third day.

Benavides wakes up in the light of a new day, still far from his bed and his wife. This time he goes barefoot, without even shielding his body from the cold; he stands up and goes right out of the room, down the hallway and the stairs, out of the house and across the garden to reach the garage. The men in blue are gone. They've hung bright halogen lights from the ceiling, and there, in the middle of the room, the open suitcase frames the coiled body of his abandoned wife.

The blow from behind is hard, on the nape of his neck, and there ends his fourth day.

Benavides wakes up on the night of the fourth day, and without hesitating he puts his feet into his shoes and leaves the room. The nighttime light shines in through the hallway windows to guide him on his gloomy tour. What brings a man like him to flee the house of his doctor at that hour of the night? Can a professional like Corrales, surely under strict orders from Donorio, refuse to let him see his wife? Were the restrictions part of a treatment of utmost rigor, a strategy to cure him from an illness, surely venereal, that brought him to hallucinate strange murders or to doubt his very own doctor? While he goes down the main stairs with painstaking care, Benavides wonders if these men want something in particular from his wife, whether for some reason they have seen in her things that they don't see in other women. Pleasant memories assault him like a wave of jealousy and desire; in the end, his wife is his wife and no one else's.

In the darkness it's hard to find the door out to the garden, where flashing signs light up the surroundings for seconds at a time. Soon he will reach the garage, he will get his wife out of there and go home with her in a taxi. So thinks Benavides until he discovers that his glory will be short-lived.

That is, until he receives, a little more to the left this time, that day's second blow to the head.

"The man's in bad shape, Corrales."

"It's the pressure. Success is not easily assimilated by small bodies, and we have to give him time."

"But the opening is tomorrow."

"And is he necessary, Donorio? Is it necessary to expose him like this?"

"Without the artist, the opening loses meaning. It's what I was talking about with context. Do you remember, Corrales?"

"Yes, of course."

"If the public recognizes themselves in the artist, the work's effect is magnified. Do the test yourself; think what would have happened if on Sunday night, instead of Benavides, the work had been brought to you by an athletic bodybuilder with long hair and stylish shoes . . ."

"No, no, of course. Don't think me stupid, either; the difference is . . . vast."

"Violent, Corrales, like the work."

On the bed, Benavides opens his eyes to find the two men in the room with him, sitting in armchairs.

"How do you feel, Benavides?"

Benavides closes his eyes.

"It seems he's regained consciousness . . ."

Benavides opens his eyes again. Dr. Corrales comes over to raise his eyelids and study his left eye.

"Perhaps he loses his memory intermittently," says Corrales as he shines the bright beam of a small flashlight into the center of a restless pupil.

"Are you feeling well, Benavides?"

Benavides screams, "I killed my wife, of my own volition and by myself!" and without taking his eyes from the men, he clutches the sweaty sheets.

Corrales makes an admonishing gesture, and his eyes meet Donorio's. Both men's thoughts hold unfocused doubts and the beginnings of disillusionment.

The finished installation galvanizes the media to announce the event. People form expectations and clamor for advance tickets. The air grows polluted with an anxious public's murmurings and rises to the ears of Benavides, who—for the fifth day in a row—wakes up in this house. What is a man like him doing in this room, so far from his home and his wife? Can a doctor like Corrales enter with a formal suit folded over his right arm and a set of clean underwear in his left, and say, "The socks will be a bit baggy, but the suit is just right for a man like you"? Corrales sits at the foot of the bed and gives the patient's legs a few pats, perhaps out of an affection that developed a while ago but of which Benavides has no memory, and finally he smiles and says things like "How well you're looking, Benavides," or "How I envy you, Benavides, an artist like yourself, on a day like today, with an eager public and the press on fire," or "Don't be nervous, there's every indication the opening will be a success." But Benavides is not happy: a night watchman, perhaps even Donorio himself, is monitoring the entrance to the garage, where his wife is waiting. It's an inaccessible zone for a body as prone to being beaten as his, and it's lit up, even in the shadows of night, with two potent spotlights at either side of the door, and, above them, bright signs that shamelessly pay homage to this kidnapping. It's gotten to the point that Benavides cannot distinguish evil intentions from good ones, or evaluate his doctor's postures with any certainty. He watches Corrales stretch the socks, and he sinks into a sudden unease.

Some hours later, doctor and patient study their suited-up bodies before the mirror.

"You see that it's your size, Benavides?"

Benavides stands motionless while Corrales adjusts his tie for him.

"Perfect." He points to their bodies in the mirror. "Just wait till the girls see you like this."

After some respectful knocks at the door they hear the voice of one of the women:

"Mr. Donorio sent me to tell you that everything is ready, but if the artist needs, he can wait."

"Not at all, let him know we'll be right down."

The room is large, but small compared with the crowd that has gathered. Many people didn't get in and are waiting in the front yard, peering through the living room windows or standing in line at the door guarded by the men in blue. Inside, with the work still hidden behind a red velvet curtain, the public's fervor grows.

Donorio takes the microphone.

"Ladies, gentlemen . . ."

The audience listens to the speaker.

"Today is a very special day, for me and for all of you . . ."

A few timid comments float up from the crowd and are lost in the thickness of a growing silence.

"Art is memorious, dear audience, and from the least likely molecules of this, our society, true artists majestically emerge. Ladies, gentlemen, scholars, I wish to introduce you to a dreamer, a friend, but above all else an artist on whom the world cannot turn its back . . . Benavides, if you would . . ."

Amid the crowd's thundering applause, pushed forward by Corrales, Benavides makes his way toward Donorio, who has accompanied his words with a gesture of welcome. When the artist ascends to the stage and discovers the audience, the audience discovers in him the candid, humble features of pure and sincere creation. An excited ovation grows. It calms, or pauses briefly, when Donorio returns to the microphone. The monologue continues, but the audience does not take their eyes from the artist, who studies the ceiling and the walls. One hundred pairs of eyes expectantly follow the creative movement of the artist, so removed from their gazes and their praise.

". . . something of the past remains in our collective memory, in the brilliant minds of our artists. Horror, hatred, death, all throb intensely in their persecuted minds . . ."

The artist discovers the large red velvet curtain to one side of the stage, behind which, one presumes, the work awaits. But what is it that so disturbs the artist? Why, in his simple, genius face, do pale glimmers of fear suddenly emerge?

"Gentlemen, ladies, what you are about to see goes beyond the superfluous emotions of common art. The work, this work, is the answer. Benavides, we're listening," says Donorio, and finally he leaves the microphone and cedes his place to the artist.

The audience waits. A man in blue runs to the microphone and lowers it to Benavides's height. Benavides looks at the microphone like someone studying the weight of a crime, its punishment. He takes three steps forward. It seems he is going to speak.

Donorio looks for the complicit gaze of Corrales, who keeps his eyes on the artist, proud, as though looking at a child who has finally become a man. Benavides turns toward the curtain, and then back toward the audience. There is a thrilling silence. Then Benavides takes the microphone and says:

"I killed her."

The message takes time to sink in. Once the audience processes the words and understands their meaning, they start slowly to applaud, moved. Euphoria breaks out. *He says he killed her*, they say to one another. *Now, that is intense*, they comment. *Pure poetry*, shouts someone in the back. The evening's first tears of emotion fall. On one side of the stage Corrales nods along with the general murmur. Donorio moves the artist aside and returns to his position. Two men in blue come onstage and stand to either side of the red cloth. And Donorio says:

"Friends, the work . . ."

And like the sun brings light or like the artist discovers the most human truths, the curtain that had covered the creation now, slowly before the collective hunger, falls to the floor. And there is the work: violent, real, carnally alive. Donorio has lost the public's attention, but even so he names it. He pronounces the title, savoring every letter:

"Violence."

And the name lands: it descends to the crowd, and the crowd explodes.

The euphoria is uncontainable. People shove, try to climb onstage. A dozen men in blue form a barrier that blocks their advance. But the audience wants to see, and the barrier gives way. Excitement. Commotion. Something emanates from that work and it drives them mad. The sovereign image of the purple body. Death a few feet away. Human flesh, human skin. Giant thighs. Coiled in a suitcase. Squeezed into the leather. And the smell. The artist is still very close to the suitcase. Too exposed. His singular face stands out in the crowd, and they discover him. There is a surprising moment. When they realize it's him, they lift him up, pass him from hand to hand. Corrales shouts: "The artist!" and some men in blue leave their human barricade to rescue Benavides. The audience, after hearing Corrales's cries, lets go of Benavides, and he is lost among the people like a pearl in muddy water. After the stillness of married life, this unprecedented experience excites him. Hidden in the crowd, concealed even from the crowd itself, he moves through the euphoric bodies toward the nucleus of the disturbance. There are shouts, shoves, people fight to get a better view. Then Benavides feels a chasm open. It opens in front of him and separates him from the rest of humanity. Corrales sees it all, because he intuits the artist's feelings. He has bet on Benavides's future. He wishes, in the small man, for a kind of discovery: the ancestral pleasure of knowing oneself a creator, anxiety contained. He wants to see Benavides's hands squeeze absent matter in the air, seek something to knead, sense the scant time and the colossal task, forget the leisurely latency of the common man. To see, before his candidly expectant eyes, the matter: dozens of bodies that throb and wait, the primordial mass to be rent, coiled, forced, to attain, majestically, under the expert hand of a practiced superior, the precise measures of the leather suitcase.

And though none of that happens, Corrales does not feel frustrated. His close relationship with human processes fills him with faith. Donorio smiles at him. Benavides, finally restrained by the custodians, withdraws through the main door.

With growing enthusiasm, everyone welcomes smiling waitresses bearing champagne. The opening has been a success.

ABOUT THE AUTHOR

Samanta Schweblin was chosen as one of the twenty-two best writers in Spanish under the age of thirty-five by *Granta* in 2010, and in 2017 she was named one of the Bogotá39 best Latin American writers under forty. Her first novel, *Fever Dream*, was shortlisted for the Man Booker International Prize in 2017. She is the author of award-winning story collections, and her stories have appeared in *The New Yorker*, *Harper's*, and elsewhere. Her work has been translated into twenty languages. Originally from Buenos Aires, she currently lives in Berlin.

ABOUT THE TRANSLATOR

Megan McDowell has translated books by Alejandro Zambra, Mariana Enriquez, Lina Meruane, and Diego Zuñiga, among others. Her translation of Zambra's novel *Ways of Going Home* won the 2013 English PEN Award for Writing in Translation, and her translation of Samanta Schweblin's first novel, *Fever Dream*, was shortlisted for the 2017 Man Booker International Prize. McDowell's story translations have appeared in *The New Yorker*, *The Paris Review*, *Harper's*, *Tin House*, *Granta*, and *Vice*, among others. She is from Kentucky and now lives in Santiago, Chile.

Also by Samanta Schweblin:

FEVER DREAM

SHORTLISTED FOR THE MAN BOOKER
INTERNATIONAL PRIZE, 2017

A young woman named Amanda lies dying in a rural hospital clinic. A boy named David sits beside her. She's not his mother. He's not her child.

The two seem anxious and, at David's ever more insistent prompting, Amanda recounts a series of events from the apparently recent past. As David pushes her to recall whatever trauma has landed her in her terminal state, he unwittingly opens a chest of horrors, and suddenly the terrifying nature of their reality is brought into shocking focus.

One of the freshest new voices writing in Spanish, Samanta Schweblin creates an aura of strange and deeply unsettling psychological menace in this cautionary tale of maternal love, broken souls and the power and desperation of family.

'Terrifying and brilliant… Dangerously addictive.'   *Guardian*